Augustus F. Lindley

The Log of the Fortuna

A Cruise on Chinese Waters

Augustus F. Lindley

The Log of the Fortuna
A Cruise on Chinese Waters

ISBN/EAN: 9783337082369

Printed in Europe, USA, Canada, Australia, Japan

Cover: Foto ©Andreas Hilbeck / pixelio.de

More available books at **www.hansebooks.com**

THE LOG
OF
THE FORTUNA.

VIEW ON THE CREEK.

THE LOG

OF

THE FORTUNA:

A Cruise on Chinese Waters.

*CONTAINING TALES OF ADVENTURE IN FOREIGN CLIMES
BY SEA AND BY SHORE.*

BY

CAPTAIN AUGUSTUS F. LINDLEY,

AUTHOR OF "'TI-PING-TIEN-KWOH,' THE HISTORY OF THE TI-PING REVOLUTION
"THEODORE'S CASE," &c. &c.

SECOND EDITION.

CASSELL, PETTER, & GALPIN,
LONDON, PARIS, AND NEW YORK.

THE LOG:

CONTAINING THE FOLLOWING TALES—

ILLUSTRATIONS.

SHANGHAI.

THE LOG OF THE "FORTUNA."

A CRUISE IN CHINESE WATERS.

"CHANGE, sir; change, or death!" So, without beating about the bush, said the doctor, one burning morning at Shanghai.

I was suffering from a multiplicity of complaints—rheumatism, fever, and ague, not to mention a pleasant suspicion of dysentery. I felt, therefore, that the verdict was a true one, and began to curse that obstinate, roving disposition of mine, which had led me, in the first place, to forsake a comfortable home and a dear wife in England,

in order to see after property at Manilla, left us by my wife's late
uncle, when an agent would have done as well; and which, in the
second place, induced me to take a trip to China, pending a long and
tedious progress of business through the Manilla courts, during which
I was not required to appear in person.

I felt bitterly annoyed to think that I had given up so much in
order to lay my bones in China—that distant, out-of-the-way, outlandish, barbarian country: that remote empire where the compass
points south instead of north; where men wear petticoats and women
wear trousers; where they shave the head instead of the chin; where
pockets are worn outside instead of inside the dress; where bed-
rooms are on the ground floor instead of up-stairs; where the men
wear pigtails, but cut off their pigs' tails; where shoes, umbrellas,
and lanterns are made of paper; where wooden anchors are used for
ships, which are built with square instead of pointed bows; where
etiquette commands people to put on the hat instead of take it off;
where they write with a paint-brush instead of a pen; where they
pray to devils much more earnestly than to gods; where rank and
title, instead of being hereditary, is retrospective, and ascends to a
man's great-grandmother, &c., instead of descending to his suc-
cessors; and where, in fact, not to write a volume of the contrariness
and difference to European taste and custom, everything is grotesque,
upside-down, and entirely opposed to western civilisation.

I fall back in bed and grievously reflect upon all these things;
and at every twinge of my rheumatism—which, by the way, is captain
and leader of my other maladies—life and prospects seem to grow
blacker and blacker.

"Boy! boy, you rascal!" I at last yell.

Several moments elapse, and then that charming youth puts in an appearance—charming youth, indeed! whose chief characteristics are determined obstinacy and preternatural cunning.

"What ting wantchee, master?"

The villain's tone is not, perhaps, the most humble, not the most civil in the world, for, in his own mind, he has long ago given me up as sure to die, and merely keeps up an *appearance* of docility.

"Boy! Doctor talkee, 'S'pose mi no walkee from Shanghai mi must die;' which place more better go?"

Boy gravely considers, and at length maketh reply—

"Pootung."

Now, "Pootung" is that low slab of black mud on the other side of the river, and immediately opposite Shanghai settlement, of which it is the "Surrey side." There, when poor "Jack" dies, he is conveyed, cased in four deal planks, and laid in the cemetery which flourishes inland, green and damp, amidst the waving, watery rice-fields. So green is that thickly-tenanted cemetery that it suggests a fertility unpleasantly accelerated.

If sarcasm *could* lurk beneath that stolid exterior, I should have called Assam's answer a masterpiece; but I hardly think it can. However, taking care to be on the right side, I almost dislocated my best arm by throwing an enormous boot at his head—missing him, of course. Once more I resign myself to meditation, and chew the cud of sweet and bitter fancies—only, alas! they are all bitter.

I had mentally completed a very fair disposition of my worldly goods and effects, till only one revolver remained. This fire-arm (patented by some tremendously long-named German, and wonderfully ornamental in appearance, but altogether unserviceable) had distinguished itself on several occasions by discharging the whole six chambers at once, and

was, in fact, almost certain death to the person firing it.   I naturally
wished to leave it to some *very* particular friend, and was thinking
over a list of them, when I became suddenly startled by a terrific
voice resounding in the courtyard of my domicile.

"Assam !" it roared.   Then a momentary interval elapsed, and
the voice bellowed forth again.   "Boy! you thundering thief!" &c.
&c. (You see, most Anglo-Saxons seem to consider that a little
vituperation in the national vernacular is always effective with people
of African or Asiatic race)   "Boy! where is your master ?"

Then boy, somewhat aghast at the wealth of the English
language in abuse, ushers in my old friend Esmond—he of the
fair-haired, Saxon *physique*, the sturdy limbs, and the loud-toned voice.

"Skulking again !" roared he (for, sailor-like, he always seems
to imagine that he is hailing some distant maintop, and speaks in a
corresponding key)—"skulking again, are you ?"

This large, cool presence, with its ponderous health and strength,
almost maddens me with jealousy.   I scowl, but answer not.   Bless
you, he does not care ; not he !

"Well, old fellow, how are you ?   Where's the brandy ?"   (I
make a motion with my finger.)   "Ah ! thank you.   Don't stir, I
have it.   And the water ?   That's right.   Boy, bring your master's
best cigars—that big box in the corner.   Poor devil !" (Esmond now
intended to be soothing), " he won't live to smoke them, and " (here
the brute thought to be witty, and pointed to the ground with one fat
finger containing almost as much blood as the whole of my body)
"down there they smoke all the time—for nothing.   Ha, ha, ha !"
Witty fellow !

"Well," continued he, when his manilla was fairly alight, " I'm
off to-morrow.   I have a good charter for the schooner - a cargo to

Ningpo, and a few friends of mine intend joining for a cruise, as I am thinking of taking a roving commission for a spell." (At this moment his eye lighted on that big boot, lying where it had fallen after missing my amiable Celestial's head.) "Ah, by-the-bye, those long boots of yours fit me to a T. I'll just tell your boy to put them into my boat, shall I?"

"Yes, certainly! Sing out for him," I reply.

Boy arrives, trembling at the yet thrilling vibration of Esmond's mighty tones, and I say—

"Look here, Assam. Pack my portmanteau. Get one case of brandy, one barrel of beer, my double-barrel gun, rifle, duck-gun, and revolvers, and put them all into Mr. Esmond's boat. Then go down town, catchee one piecee cask of soda-water, and make chin-chin your smallo piecee wifo, for one moon or so. Qui, qui (quick, quick), now! And, boy, put those too muchee large piecee boots in the *sanpan* too." ("I shall want them to shoot in," I explain to the astounded Esmond.) "Ah! and that medicine! take it to that piecee doctor man, Mr. Jones" (the friend to whom I had determined to bequeath the elaborate German revolver), "with my best compliments, and he may find it useful."

Then I sit up in bed, and grin horribly at the awe-stricken Esmond, who thinks, I am sure, by the peculiar expression of his great, good-natured countenance, that my vitality is having a feeble little flickering before total extinction; then I groan out, "Ho! for the *Fortuna*, and a yachting cruise."

"Well!" he at length managed to ejaculate, "I need not say how heartily welcome you will be; but, my dear fellow" (and I saw two large tears, one glistening in each corner of his large blue eyes), "my dear fellow! do you think that you will live to get aboard?"

Dear old Esmond! He was a warm, open-hearted fellow, though he *did* ask for my boots. Alas! he had seen so many dear friends breathe their last in that undermining, diabolical Chinese climate, that such things had become quite every-day events, and he seemed, with his unassailable iron constitution, to be destined to bury all who knew him.

In the cool of the evening my boy duly announced that a sedan was in waiting. Boy is not very amiable in manner, for his Celestial understanding plainly telleth him that this yachting trip will most materially interfere with those little plans that he had cunningly formed with regard to my valuables, in case of my death at Shanghai. I suffer myself to be carried out and placed in the conveyance. The bearers—during the half-hour they waited in the court-yard—have, with Chinese ingenuity, been minutely discussing my chances of life. I can see it by their looks—by the twinkle in their little oblique black eyes. They are perfectly acquainted with the nature of my ailments, and bump me twice as much as they would have done had I not been such a martyr to rheumatism. I think they are seeking a secret sort of patriotic revenge for the capture of the "Summer Palace" at Pekin. They also covertly grin to each other, and improvise an unusually melancholy dirge as they trot me away down the *bund*.

On that broad promenade we meet many acquaintances, and more than one pale-faced lady, sauntering languidly along in search of cooling breezes from the river, but finding, I fear, only warm puffs of heavily-laden air, redolent of dead drowned Chinamen who daily float down with the tide.

Arrived at the jetty, abreast of which the good schooner *Fortuna* lies moored, Esmond lifts me out of the chair into his *sanpan* (*lit.*, three planks), or sculling-boat, which boat resembles nothing in the world so much as half a walnut-shell, except, indeed, a whole one, when the mats that form the awning are drawn close over.

By a series of sickly rolls or plunges we fetch alongside the schooner, and I am hoisted on deck.

"Welcome aboard the *Fortuna*," cries Esmond.

His vessel is as dainty a little clipper as one could wish to set eyes on; black, sharp, and rakish in hull and spars; clean and spotlessly white about her decks. She is heavily armed, too, with a couple of pivot eighteen-pounders, and a twelve-pounder bow-chaser on the forecastle.

Crawling down into the cabin, I pass on the way a very elaborate pantry; and a glimpse of what it contains seems to enliven me. I see cases marked "Martell," "Hennessey," "V. H. D.," "Crosse and Blackwell," "Fortnum and Mason," "Moet," "Bass," "Guinness," &c. &c. &c.; also, cunningly-shaped bottles suggestive of schnaps and "cock-tails," burly hams and sweet-smelling sides of English bacon; whilst the pleasant sound of lively poultry is wafted to my ears, and follows me, as with an outcry against my intended consumption of chicken-broth, to my sick couch on the transoms.

Some dozen highly-polished "Enfields" are ranged round the cool, Indian-matted cabin. The skylight admits a refreshing sea breeze, just beginning to blow up the river; above all—before all—suspended to the upper deck beams, hang two red, porous, clay "chatties," which I well know contain water—cool, delicious, icy water.

As the evening advanced, I began to feel better than I had done for many a day. The change from the hot, dry, parched, and comfortless shore, to the cooling, pleasant life on the water already had its effect. As the time drew near at which Esmond expected his friends to come on board, I induced him to place a stuffed silk mattress, covered with Madras matting, under the quarter-deck awning; and upon this luxuriant couch I sank down with a sigh of satisfaction, like some worn-out, sensual old Turk.

Assam, still with a lowering sulkiness in his looks, brought "brandy pawnee," and aromatic cheroots, with a large piece of slow-burning scented "joss-stick" glowing on a tray.

It is a cool, clear, beautiful night. For the first time I admire Shanghai. Its many lights on the shore-line, the gleam of the moon on the white walls of its houses, the looming of the Chinese-built, fantastic-shaped Custom House, the shaded tracing of the numerous vessels all around, the pleasing sound of the infinitely various-toned ship-bells striking in every direction as each half-hour arrives. are all objects that a thoughtful observer cannot fail to appreciate.

Regularly our old Manilla quartermaster paces the deck and strikes the sweet-toned bell. Esmond and I quaff grog, and yarn, and grow quite sentimental. The sparkling stars, or worlds, shining down upon us from their distant homes, myriads and myriads of miles away in that blue, illimitable, boundless space above; the stately ships, floating so strongly, so buoyantly upon that gurgling tide, and soon to bear far away to the uttermost parts of the earth precious freights from the groaning storehouses of that vast emporium ashore, where Commerce—that mighty king—is gradually drawing the most opposite races nearer together in the bonds of universal brotherhood, by slowly, silently, but still surely, introducing the effect, if not the actual practice and principle, of Christian civilisation—these were subjects sufficiently attractive to produce the feast of reason and the flow of wit. I rather think that most of the talking fell to my share, for good old Esmond was far more matter-of-fact than imaginative, and could

THE "FORTUNA" AT SHANGHAI.

discuss the trim of a ship far better than he could understand the enunciation of an abstruse metaphysical problem, or comprehend the formidable thesis of some terribly learned and dogmatical theologian. As for his knowledge of the physical sciences, he knew how to work his vessel's reckoning, and he knew that a rock was a hard substance —harder than wood—to be carefully avoided by those who went down to the sea in ships, and saw the wonders of the deep.

Suddenly the quartermaster broke in upon my enthusiasm by gruffly hailing an approaching boat—

" Boat, ahoy !

" Halloo ! " came echoing back a still rougher and more sailor-toned reply.

" What boat is that ? " cried the quartermaster.

" Passengers coming aboard," roared a voice that excelled even Esmond's, and which made the latter exclaim—

" I'll be keelhauled if that is not old Jack Backstay ! "

The next moment the *sanpan* grated alongside, and a stout, short, thick-set, brawny figure came up the side, hand over hand, rolled up to us, and, seizing my friend by the hand, roared out—

" Well, Esmond, my boy-ee ! what cheer, what cheer ? "

I at once found out where my friend had derived his habit of stentorian shouting from. This was Jack Backstay, and Jack Backstay had been chief mate of every ship in which Esmond had served his apprenticeship to the sea. After this old-fashioned specimen of a thorough British mercantile marine officer had brought himself to an anchor by our side, he explained the circumstances to which we were indebted for his visit. He had lately arrived in Shanghai, had left his ship, was now out of a berth, and having heard of the intended pleasure trip, came off to join in it, being sure of a hearty welcome from the boy he had himself made "a man and a sailor"—as he was fond of saying.

Two pale-faced individuals followed Mr. Backstay up the gang-way ladder, the first being Dr. O'Kilorkure, who no sooner reached the deck than he thrust his head over the rail, and sang out---

"Hoy! you *sanpan* man, bring up that case of instruments. Take care! take care you do not drop them, bad luck to ye! Sure, now, you'll be afther losing thim!"

Up came a Shanghai boatman, carefully carrying the doctor's case : fine fellows, those Shanghai watermen—strong, muscular, hard-working fellows as one could anywhere find, but terrible rogues, though, as a rule, if kindly treated or well acquainted with any exiled European, faithful and true to the backbone.

Eagerly grasping his instruments, the doctor came aft. I had never seen him before, and, being sick, I must confess my wishes were that I might never see him again. I knew at once that the man was almost a monomaniac at least, and that his mania was amputation. He was a tall, bony, sanguine-complexioned, genuine Irishman.

Slowly, leisurely, and languidly the last passenger came over the gangway. He was a man of dollars, of hearty English style, but of great liver, and sickly appearance. That mighty dollar! How many noble spirits become contaminated, how many patient friends at home become desolate evermore, through the blind infatuation of those who will not return to their native land with what they have made, but who struggle against ill-health and a sickly climate, till death comes to end their useless toiling for more! more! more! Where are the limits to human ambition and desire? Alas! that Pootung Cemetery gives a mute but ghastly sarcastic reply.

Mr. Lawrence had a large mercantile concern, any amount of credit among the Chinese native merchants, and was quite rich enough to have retired to England with a comfortable competency ; but to every friendly remonstrance replied, " Oh, the mail after next, the mail after next, I shall certainly go home." They say, " to-morrow never comes." Certainly Mr. Lawrence was a living verifica-tion of the adage. The next mail never came, to my knowledge ; but I feel sure that he must have had some good reason for wishing to increase his wealth, for he was a kind, earnest philanthropist.

Our party of five were soon upon the most intimate and friendly terms, quaffing our grog—at least, I was not, for one glass formed my allowance—smoking our fragrant manillas, yarning of home, and friends, and happy days, and well-known scenes far, far away, to which we all felt a strong hope that we might some day return. I cannot exactly say how it was, but certainly the glances of that Hibernian medico seemed to make me get better. I felt morally persuaded that if the fellow only once heard me complain of a pain in my leg or arm, his native blarney would convince my friends, and I should perforce become a subject for his horrid pet knives and saws. For-tunately for me, Dr. O'Kilorkure was a great talker ; he was very fond of hearing the sound of his own voice ; and every one was really charmed to listen to his flowing, bright, impassioned eloquence. His was a singular case of mistaken vocation ; he should have been a leader in the House of Commons at least.

January 1st.

The sea log of the *Fortuna* commences this day.

About 5*h. a.m.* my boy brought me a strong cup of coffee, with a *petite verre* of cognac—a wise precaution in a cholera country. A few minutes later Esmond's roar from his state-room on the starboard side of the cabin informs me that we are about to get under weigh.

From my coign of vantage beneath the awning I complacently survey this proceeding. Old Jack Backstay is pacing to and fro the quarter-deck as though he had just relieved the officer of the watch on board his own ship—so strong is habit, especially with an old salt; if, as Mr. Backstay used to say, "they have nothing else to do and can't sleep," they are sure to be taking that circumscribed but interminable quarter-deck march. As for our two long-shore companions, they are still fast asleep in their berths below.

The capstan is manned, and we commence heaving in our chain cable. The good Chinese mariners, our crew, do not seem to believe in hard work, so, in spite of Esmond's long legs and arms—which fly about in a manner almost miraculous—it is a slow business ; so slow, indeed, that we just manage to lose the tide, and, by some mysterious means, an anchor also. The day is wasted in futile attempts to recover the lost anchor and cable. Sunset approaches. We quietly let go another bower, pay out thirty fathoms of chain, and make all snug for the night. This our tars had evidently foreseen, and are therefore by no means disconcerted.

January 2nd.

Our seamen are away in the small boat, looking for the buoy attached to our lost anchor and cable. So long do they stay that Mr. Backstay shrewdly observes he is inclined to think the bight of the chain has drifted into an opium-shop ashore. Upon communicating his fears on the subject to our host and captain, the latter thinks it more than probable. He sends his boy ashore to look for them, and, after several hours' search, the latter returns on board

CREEK WHERE THE CREW WERE FOUND.

with the information that he had succeeded in finding them comfortably bestowed, and smoking opium at the opium-shop upon the banks of the strange little creek shown by the accompanying illustration.

About 6*h.* *p.m.*, the crew return, calm and collected one and all, and vow that they cannot find the cable. Esmond wishes to know "why?" They smile placidly, and "don't know." Esmond waxes vicious. The crew get more and more composed; they don't *say*, but they evidently *mean*, "don't care." Esmond kicks them all round for lying and skulking.

8*h.* *p.m.*—Tremendous row forward. Manilla quartermaster gives me his arm; then Esmond and myself proceed to the scene of action, expecting to find murder and sudden death at least. Are disappointed. It is only A-sing abusing A-look, A-look's father, mother, grandfather, grandmother, and whole line of ancestry, from the very first down to the very last. A-look retaliates. The friends of one party curse friends of other party, and other party's fathers, mothers, and ancestors. But there are neither blows, nor any probability of them. Esmond administers sundry hard knocks and kicks, with language to match, and there is peace—for a time, the row being resumed at intervals during the night. Indeed, they wake up about every two hours, abuse each other with revigorated energy, and then go to sleep again. Evidently they must have either eaten or imbibed something which disagrees with them.

January 3rd.

This day we formed and set the watches, "ship-shape and Bristol fashion," as our weather-beaten friend, Jack Backstay, said. Esmond and myself composed the starboard watch; Mr. Backstay took charge of the port, which included the two landsmen.

C

It is my pleasing duty to record the fact that our seamen made quite a Sabbath of this day also ; returning, after dusk, satisfied but unsuccessful.   A Chinese swell, one of the owners of the cargo, came on board at 9*h.* *p.m.*   This good person understands his countrymen better than we do, for he ought to have been on board two days ago, but assures us he was quite sure that the schooner would not get away at the time advertised, as such would not be " Chinese fashion"—to do anything in a hurry, I presume. This gentleman is partial to cherry brandy, and finishes two bottles of that liquid without apparent effort.

January 4th.

Esmond sends the two Manilla quartermasters in the boat with the crew, and in an hour they return with the end of the cable. We get the anchors up, and then commence dropping down to Woo-sung, at the mouth of the Shanghai river, eleven miles distant.   It is wonderful with what skill the Chinese manage this operation, though not without their favourite noise.

6*h. p.m.*—Arrive at Woo-sung.   A large Shantung wood junk being anchored close astern, we hail her crew to shift her helm. They won't.   We foul her.   This does not at all discompose our *lowder* (Chinese captain) ; he calls for an axe, gives three chops on the grass cable of the junk, and that vehicle, released from restraint, floats gently away down the river, without her crew seeming the least aware of what had happened.   This incident is so purely Chinese as to cause no remark.

January 5th.

Esmond gives orders for the preparation of a great dinner,

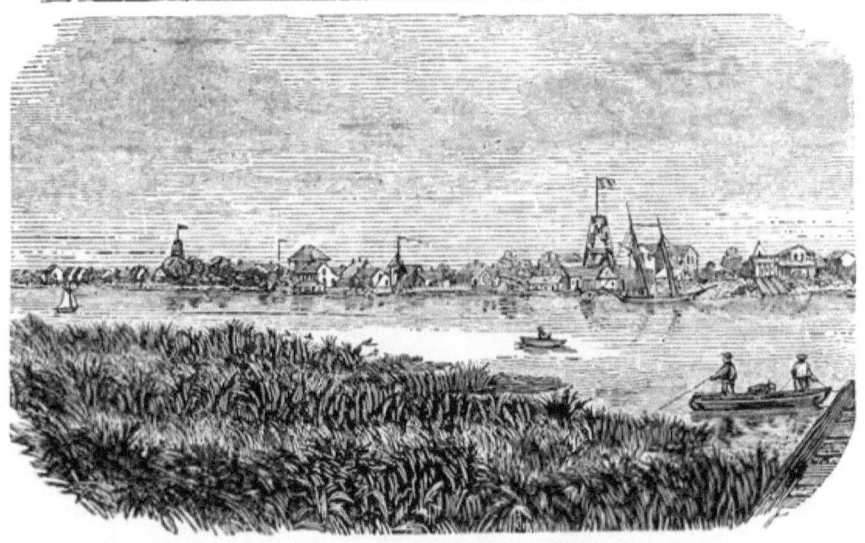

PART OF FRENCH "CONCESSION," AT WOO-SUNG.

as (he says) it is his birthday. I am inclined to think that my friend's birthdays are pleasing hallucinations, for, to my certain knowledge, he has had as many as six in one year. Almost as bad as my boy Assam, whose mother (rest her soul!) has expired seventeen times since he entered my service—a melancholy event, necessitating the granting of several days' leave for him to attend the funeral ceremonies. I have no doubt—if he is fortunate—that the old lady will die seventeen times more before he leaves me.

Another Chinese incident is noted this day. The cook comes aft with a deplorably lugubrious expression of countenance, and in his out-stretched hands we see three of his master's fowls, which he declares, in a most painfully solemn and sorrowful manner, he found dead in the hencoop. He wishes to know what shall be done with

them.   Esmond orders them to be thrown overboard.   I watch.
Cook slyly takes them to his friends, the crew.   Upon investigating
the matter we discover that those gentry had done the wretched
birds to death by boring their heads with a pin, well knowing that
the " Yang-quitzos " (*i.e.*, "foreign devils," the polite generic term
for all Europeans and people outside China) will not eat anything
that dies a natural death.

Noon.—We go ashore, Esmond and I.   Nothing very remarkable about Woo-sung, except that the French tricolour waves over the
" Joss-house ; " and the town—which commands the river—seems to
be in the occupation of a strong detachment of Chasseurs d'Afrique,
sturdy specimens of whom roll about the streets in a state of vinous
excitement, and knock down, if they do not rob, after the usual
manner of those placid warriors whether in the territory of friend or
foe, any inhabitants unfortunate enough to get in their way.   There
is something up at Woo-sung ; ten years more, or less, may see the
French claim it as their own.   A great deal might be said about
the peculiar policy that nation is pursuing in China.   They have
inserted the thin edge of the wedge of occupation in more than
one of the treaty ports—to wit, Shanghai, Ningpo, Cheefoo.   We
pretty well know that in *La belle France* there is a long-headed
carpenter who wields the hammer.   The French, be it observed,
prefer the word " concession " to the word " settlement " in the
matter of land not their own.

H.M.S. ——.   Bound in.   We dip our ensign, but the naval
grandees, with a courtesy truly British, make no reply, and take no
notice of us.

January 6th.

4*h. a.m.*—Up anchor.   Make all sail, and stand out to sea

with a fair wind.   Slight swell on.   As a consequence, our non-nautical passengers, as well as the native charterers, are in a state necessitating the presence of the steward, who rushes to and fro, holding white *amphoræ*.   Our unfortunate friends have not got their sea-legs aboard, and are holding on "by their eyebrows." With every lee-lurch they utter doleful sounds; with every weather-roll they fetch way and sprawl about ; with every plunge they seem like to die. As for the charterers, we must except them from the comforts of the cabin. Being Chinese, they retire to the lower regions, and are ill, without comfort or attendance.   The schooner is lively, and our two friends are rolling and floundering about in the midst of every movable article. Beds, blankets, boxes, packages, basins, glasses, &c., are flying around them, whilst over all prevails the odour of brandy and sea-sickness.

I am greatly improved in health, able to enjoy my dinner, and laugh at the hapless landsmen.

5h. p.m.—A very suspicious-looking native craft works up from under our lee, until she gains the weather-gage of us, and then dodges quietly along on our beam. We depress one of the eighteen-pounders. Charterer, between violent attacks of nausea, swears it is a pirate, and implores us to fire.   We do not.   In a little while the stranger puts her helm hard up, and goes dead away to leeward.   She was only a pirate having a "look see," and must have discovered that we were a customer with ugly big teeth.

8h. p.m.—Esmond, enveloped in a shaggy monkey-jacket, with a bottle of brandy, a brace of revolvers, and unlimited comforters, goes on deck to keep the first watch.

Midnight.—Esmond, with a remarkably red nose, calls me, and I turn out and go on deck, the sickness of our friends having altered the arrangement of the watches.

OUR "LOWDER" AND HIS WIFE AT OPIUM.

January 7th.

1*h. a.m.*—It appears that I had just dozed off to sleep in my watch—the schooner, for all purposes of navigation, being in the hands of the Chinese *lowder*—when I was suddenly aroused by the noise of the anchor being let go, and the sound of the cable whizzing out "at the rate of knots." Presently, however, a Chinese bend, or fastening, about four feet in circumference, catching in the hawse-pipe—which is only a foot wide—snap goes the chain, and another anchor (with some twenty fathoms of cable) is added to the treasures of the deep.

The *lowder*, good man! preserves his equanimity, lets go the other anchor, lowers the mainsail, and proceeds to his virtuous couch, his wife (whom he is allowed to have on board), and his opium pipes; impressed, no doubt, with the serious conviction that he has done his duty like a (China) man.

I take the bearings of the headlands in sight, and find that we are very nearly upon a nasty mud-bank. Chapu and Hang-chow lay west of us; off both places the tide runs like a sluice, sometimes at the extraordinary velocity of ten knots an hour! As the schooner was yawing about in a curious manner, I gave her a sheer with the helm; then, finding that she rode more quietly to her anchor, went below to turn in; but, before doing so, placed one of the Manilla quartermasters on the look-out.

I had just gone comfortably to sleep, when the noise of heaving in cable awoke me. I rushed on deck, to find the anchor off the ground, and two large boats, under sail, standing towards us from the shore. Our Chinese mariners were hailing these boats, and, as I knew they were not to be trusted, I sang out for Esmond. Directly he appeared we beat to quarters. Our fighting force consisted of five Europeans and two Manilla men: these latter may have been good men and true, but, I am free to confess, they looked very much like superannuated Greenwich pensioners, who had been embalmed in coffee-grounds and dug up when wanted.

We cast loose the after gun, and gave the nearest boat a dose of grape-shot without any preamble. Hardly had the report died away when splash went our anchor once more. The schooner gave, whilst swinging, a terrific bump, and we knew that we were ashore. As for the supposed pirates, we see that they are flying, with the proverbial insect in their ear. We load again, nevertheless, and look round for the Celestial portion of our crew. They have vanished below, permitting us either to do the fighting or leave it alone, one

thing only being patent to their limited capacity—viz., that it is not
their *pidgin* (business) to bark or bite.

Esmond is not naturally of the most gentle temperament, and
this last proceeding of his mariners—though strictly in accordance
with the precepts of one Dr. Watts—provokes his wrath.   He
descends to his cabin; reappearing with a keen-edged, two-handed
Japanese sword.   I arm myself with a revolver; the Manilla quartermasters have their knives; and, leaving our three friends in charge
of the deck, we go forward to drive up our recreant crew, not
knowing but what some treachery might be afloat.   Most of them
return pretty quickly to the deck, though not all, so Esmond dives
down below, flourishing his deadly weapon.   One unfortunate, either
more obstinate or less active than his compeers, fails to follow them.
Him Esmond chases; both uttering startling yells.   At last the
pursuer, in an unwary moment, puts his foot into a deep hole and
falls, giving the terrified Celestial time to reach the upper regions.
The Manilla men view him gloomily, muttering sundry *carrambas*
but not doing anything desperate, being themselves of a rather
dilapidated, not to say antiquated, build, and scarcely up to any
violent physical exertion.

Esmond soon follows his late antagonist, who, seeing danger
still looming, covers himself with his quilt, and flies aft so swiftly
that the skipper relinquishes all further idea of catching him and
inflicting exemplary punishment.

The crew are certainly sulky, but we soon restore discipline.
Unavailingly, we try every means to get the schooner off the mud-
bank.   I must again record my admiration of the resigned behaviour
of the whole body of Chinese seamen—from the *lowdar* to the
smallest boy.

THE "FORTUNA" ASHORE.

3h. a.m.—Tide falling. Water rapidly shoaling. No more sleep for us this morning. Daylight breaks, and we find ourselves in a curious position. On the starboard hand there is mud, on the port hand there is mud; mud ahead, mud astern; below is mud; and a muddy-coloured sky is frowning above. Water there is, in muddy little rivulets—the ocean, no!

The ebb tide has left us high and dry indeed, the sea in this place retiring in a body. But a few moments before there was water enough to float us, and now there is not enough to swim a lucifer-match.

But though water is scarce, there are plenty of fishermen about —strange parties, wild-looking and long-haired. Gaunt athletes, whose sinews and muscles would not have disgraced a Roman amphi-theatre; and their clothing being of the airiest, we have an excellent opportunity to judge. Here and there they have a small canoe, but they are principally paddling about on the mud, wearing a curious kind of shoe, which enables them to glide along the slippery surface at a great speed, and carrying long, narrow-bladed spades, with which to dig up worms, shell-fish, edible roots, and other things peculiar to Chinese mud. Those who come near are civil, for they notice the seven "foreign devils" (the Manilla men, despite any small physical infirmity, being counted as bonâ fide "Yang-quitzos" by the natives); but if only one white man had been on board the *Fortuna*, the night dark, and the vessel in serious trouble, how would they have behaved? I can guess—somewhat piratically and murderously.

At breakfast this morning we discuss our position. The *lowder*, the charterers, every Chinaman on board, all declare that it will be impossible to get the schooner off for four or five days to come, until higher tides set in. There is no help for it, so we make ourselves contented; organise shooting parties, for the shoals and indentations along the coast abound with wild fowl; retain several of the amphibious fishermen with their canoes, so that we can go fishing, and, in fact, do all we can to enjoy ourselves—to eat, drink, and be merry.

January 8th.

This day I propose that we shall relieve the singing, card-playing, smoking, and imbibing, wherewith we pass the long evenings, by story-telling, or rather, to be nautically correct, by spinning yarns. Esmond and the rest applaud the idea, and cheer-

SPINNING OUR YARNS.

fully respond to it. Kind reader! may we hope that you will do likewise? It was settled that we should commence our tales that night, and that Esmond, as host and captain, should lead off. We agreed that each of us should spin a yarn, and it was arranged that Mr. Lawrence should follow Esmond on the second night, I on the third, Dr. O'Kilorkure on the fourth, and old Jack Backstay on the fifth, by which time we hoped to be clear of the mud-bank; but, should that not prove to be the case, as I had started the story-telling, and it was a thing more in my way than in my friend's, it was further arranged that I should tell a second tale.

Promptly as the bell struck eight that night we all assembled round the cheerful stove in the after part of the cabin. The great swinging lamp was sufficiently removed to give just the sort of subdued light most pleasant, and which neither overpowered the thought-inspiring, dull red flashes proceeding from the glowing embers, nor the tall, fantastic shadows dancing and playing with such silent but contented humour all around. The darkest corners of the cabin seemed full of sporting little imps; and those shadowy forms, giving life to our wooden walls, might well have been taken for an assemblage of orderly spirits of the air, anxious to hear our yarns.

The punch being brewed, the box of fragrant manillas placed near at hand, and our five selves comfortably stretched around, in easy-chairs, on sofas, or the soft-cushioned transom lockers, Esmond, after a few preliminary observations, began his yarn, which was no other than the narration of an adventure he had himself experienced in China.

THE "QUEEN MARY."

The Schooner Skipper's Yarn.

AN ADVENTURE ON THE YANG-TSE-KIANG.
A PERILOUS EXPLOIT IN CHINA.

My *Queen Mary* was a smart little *lorcha* of one hundred tons burden, and, shortly before the great river, the Yang-tse-Kiang (*i.e.*, the "Son of the Sea," as the natives have poetically named it), was opened to foreigners by the jealous Government of China, I was foolish enough to venture on a trading trip up its almost unknown, and comparatively unexplored waters.

If the dangers of such a voyage were great, the profits, we knew, would be proportionately large. We were tired of the Ningpo and coasting trade, at which we could now scarcely make the expenses of our vessel ; and so, altogether, pocket overcame prudence, and away we went, bound for the rich, unknown, and therefore tempting regions of the Yang-tse-Kiang.

Besides myself and partner, Frank Travers, who owned half the *lorcha*, our crew consisted of Hans, an immensely powerful Dutch mariner whom we had shipped as mate ; Ramah, a native of Madras, engaged as a sort of Jack-of-all-trades, or supernumerary, to increase our strength in foreigners ; my Chinese servant, or boy, aged fifty, or thereabouts, properly named A-yow, but more generally known as the "Angel" (to be read " ironical," as Artemus Ward would have said), a sobriquet to which the positive ugliness of the poor fellow had given rise some years before, when I, his master, chanced to be in a playful and sarcastic humour at the time of engaging him ; and, lastly, the *Queen Mary's* comprised our Chinese *lowder*, or captain, and twenty of his countrymen as sailors.

These tars and their long-tailed leader had been strongly recommended to me by native merchants, friends of mine, at Shang-hai, who knew them well, and had often employed them on river voyages ; thus, naturally enough, despite our experience of the treacherous Celestial nature, we thought that they could be depended upon. In the sequel it will be seen how greatly we were mistaken, how nearly we lost both vessel and valuables, and how narrowly any of my party of foreigners escaped with life. Even at this lapse of time, I can hardly think of that one dreadful night, on which occurred the terrible adventure I am about to narrate, without feeling a sort of shudder at the recollections awakened.

I must now mention an important fact—a circumstance, indeed, that eventually proved the preservation of myself. The *lowder* brought on board with him a daughter. This was much against the wish of Frank and myself; but then he would not come without her, and, sooner than lose the chance of shipping him (so unusually good

BUSH ISLAND AND MOUTH OF THE YANG-TSE-KIANG.

were his recommendations), we yielded, and even allowed the *Mys-ter-le*—Chinese carpenter—to fit up a little private cabin for her use.

The very fact of the old fellow's evidently strong attachment to his motherless daughter gave us a good opinion of his character.

Sailing up the "Son of the Sea" was at this time a venture of no little risk, for its numerous branches, creeks, and lakes were known to be pretty thickly infested with both pirates and Imperial war-junks, between whom there existed but little difference, in so far

PAWN-FUIN-SHAN, OR THE "SPLIT HILL"

as plundering propensities and murderous proclivities were concerned. Some few miles within the embouchure of the mighty Yang-tse-Kiang, and where, leaving Shanghai, we enter upon it abreast of Bush Island, that magnificent river is at least twenty miles straight across from bank to bank. In fact, except on fine clear days, the northern shore cannot be discerned from Bush Island. Then, immediately upon entering the river, we were cut off from all communication with friends, and were thrown entirely on our own devices and resources; moreover, pirates or war-junks could attack us at discretion, for we had no right upon the Yang-tse-Kiang, the treaty of Tien-tsin, which gave the authority, not being yet thought of, unless indeed in the brain of some clever diplomat, busy brewing at the war cauldron.

Nevertheless, having gone unscathed through many a perilous adventure both by land and water in that strange Celestial clime, we laughed to scorn the fearful prognostications of friends at Shanghai; besides, the trim *Queen Mary* was very well armed, carrying two long twelve-pounders as pivot-guns amidships, besides six carronades of the same calibre, three on either side, and a plentiful supply of ammunition and small arms.

The early part of the voyage proved highly prosperous and remunerative.

The river scenery was magnificent, as the accompanying sketch of Pawn-pien-shan, or the "Split Hill," will show. This wild and picturesque spot is at the commencement of the mountainous part of the river, four hundred miles inland. The weather was charming, pirates invisible, and the few war-junks that we had yet seen peaceable; so that, by the time we came to Kwa-chow—a large village five hundred miles from the sea—and where we converted the last of

our cargo into cash, all expectation of danger or trouble with the
natives had quite vanished from our minds.

By this time a great friendship—if not, indeed, a warmer feeling
—had arisen between the fair Se-she, the *lowder's* daughter, and myself.

She was a beautiful young creature, and had barely seen her
fifteenth summer; but then, in that warm eastern clime, adolescence

SE-SHE.

comes much earlier than in our colder northern
latitude. Her complexion was very fair for
a Chinese—some of whom, however, are
very beautiful—and thus presented all the
greater advantage of contrast to her luxuriant raven tresses and deep black eyes,
which, shaded by a fringe of long drooping
lashes, were wonderfully eloquent and expressive; now sparkling with passion, now
melting with tenderness, and often glancing
with a timid fawn-like sensitiveness; they
were, moreover, straight, large, and almond-shaped, with scarcely
a trace of the common Celestial obliqueness; but then, her mother
had been a native of Honan, the central province of China, where
most of the women have eyes exquisite as those of their sisters of
Spain. This beautiful young girl was of a warm, ardent, and unso-
phisticated nature; she was, indeed, the very ideal of an uncontami-
nated desert flower; the very creature of impulse. In figure she was
rather above the medium height of her countrywomen, and of a form
so lithe—of swelling, undulating proportions, so exquisitely graceful—
that I have never yet seen its equal in civilisation. Of course she had
not the fashionable cramped " small feet;" neither, fortunately, knew
she of corset nor crinoline. There was a depth of feeling, a ray

of warm, romantic, yet undeveloped sentiment in her ever expressive glorious black eyes, that at once strongly attracted my sympathies.

I had been years from England, and had not seen anything like such feminine beauty since leaving; no wonder it affected me. I cannot help describing her, for she saved my life, poor darling! but lost her own in the generous, gallant, loving act!

From the peculiar construction of the *lorcha's* cabin, I often managed to steal a few moments of Se-she's time, unobserved by her father at his station at the helm.

Our friendship commenced by the meeting of our eyes, and, after the first glance, became increased, somehow, by others not so timid, and expressing more interest. Then the fair young creature came to mend my things, having seen me, one day, botching at some ruins left by the destroying Chinese washerwomen, when, in soft and musical accents, she offered to relieve me from the task.

Sometimes I lent her books with illustrations, and, once or twice, managed to remain long enough in her company to try and explain the meaning of the strange pictures. But, as a rule, I found the old clothes serve as an excuse to be near her; and often would I sit on the deck close by, watching the silky lashes and downcast eyes, which ever and anon would be lifted just a little to give me a soft, thrilling glance.

I know not how all this would have ended, for we were fast getting in love, and by the glitter of the *lowder's* eyes and the frown on his brow, whenever he saw me near his daughter, he would evidently disapprove of our feelings if he knew them, when we came to Kwa-chow, and the catastrophe ensued.

There being any quantity of game in the neighbourhood—the swamps, marshes, creeks, and lagoons inland abounding with wild fowl, whilst pheasants, pigeons, rabbits, and musk deer were plentiful on the dry land—early one cool and frosty morning I started on a shooting excursion, accompanied by Hans and Ramah, Frank and the "Angel" remaining on board to take care of the *lorcha*.

The early winter air was delightful, and we had a capital day's sport—so much so, indeed, that we were obliged to hire a couple of natives from a small village to assist the solitary member of our Chinese crew whom we had brought to carry the game.

It was getting dusk when we began to approach Kwa-chow on our return, and I know not how to explain the chill presentiment, the sudden dread of some impending calamity that came upon me at the very instant we turned homewards. Perhaps the electro-biologists can elucidate the psychological mystery when they hear how very soon and fatally my presentiment of evil became verified. Moreover, another strange fact to be remembered is, that some unaccountable impulse caused me to look at my watch when first the indefinite dread came to my mind. I noticed that the time was exactly six o'clock.

In the course of an hour or so we came to a little wood outside Kwa-chow.

We had just entered the narrow path between the trees and bushes, when a white female form suddenly sprang up from a dark spot where it had been lying hidden, and flew towards me.

I suppose that the strange working of my mind had made me somewhat nervous, for I had long since become too hardy to feel any agitation at even the most sudden and dangerous surprises, yet, on the present occasion, my first feeling was undoubtedly one of alarm.

However, my fear was quickly allayed, and succeeded by intense amazement, for it was Se-she, who rushed into my arms, laid her hand on my shoulder, and, sobbing violently the while, poured forth such

SE-SHE COMES TO WARN US.

rapid and broken exclamations in her native tongue that I could not understand a word she said.

It seemed that Ramah (who spoke Chinese perfectly) and the sailor comprehended what she said, for the latter interrupted her, took hold of one of her arms, and tried to get her away from me; whilst the Indian, giving a loud exclamation of anger and surprise, threw down the buck he had been carrying, and looked to his arms.

I struck the Chinaman's hand from the excited girl, ordered him to be quiet, and asked her what had occurred.

The sailor at once ran off in the direction of the village; but Ramah, bounding over the ground with great leaps like a tiger, was after him, and in a couple of moments was back by my side, coolly wiping his keen *tulwar* on a large banana leaf.

"Good heavens, Ramah! what have you done?" I cried: "you have killed the man!"

"Bode ar-char (very good) Sahib," replied he, placidly. "Ramah know. Ramah heart inside berry too much sore. De soosti-wallah Chi-ne-man on board have been kill Travers Sahib; have been take de *lorcha;* have——"

"Dowse my toplights!" roared Hans, interrupting him. "D'ye mean do zay, Misder Calashe, as how dere ist a mudiny aboard?"

"Saar! no call me calashe," said Ramah, indignantly. "I no b'long Lascar sailor-man. I high caste man; before *sowar* in Fane Sahib horse!"

"Silence!" I cried. "No wrangling now. Look to your arms, and let us be ready for the worst."

Then, in the still night air, the voice of my poor Se-she was heard, sobbing—

"Oh, Ha-le!" (so she pronounced my Christian name), "Oh,

Ha-le! Gno-te foo yiu-shar Fa-lank!" (my father has killed Frank!)

In the deep silence that followed this startling announcement I could hear the hasty, excited breathing of my two followers ; but as for the coolies carrying the game, they had seated themselves on the ground near by, and, having produced their pipes, were smoking with a stolidity and indifference perfectly diabolical.

With her arms round my neck the poor girl told me all that had happened. How her father, in concert with the petty Mandarin of the place and his dozen *braves,* had led the crew to mutiny, had cut down Frank and the "Angel," and had proceeded to ransack my cabin, possessing themselves of all the money—about seven thousand dollars. Having heard that we were to be killed and put out of the way on our return, she had stepped ashore and hidden herself to watch for our coming, so as to warn me of the infernal conspiracy against our lives.

We were in a terrible fix. Here we were, right in the heart of China, our vessel captured, our friend murdered, and his murderers waiting to serve us in the same manner !

No doubt the money had proved too great a temptation, and, for the sake of obtaining it, our *lowder* and crew had entered into alliance with the Mandarin of the place and his *braves.*

We had lost friends under similar circumstances, and knew that many an unfortunate white man had been killed by the Chinese for the sake of much less money than would be made by our death.

However, there was not a moment to lose in taking action of some sort, for even now a party of the bloodthirsty *braves* and muti- neers might be searching ashore for us ; or, perhaps, they might make off with the *lorcha,* and so at once deprive me of my property and cut off our only means of escape—for, unless we could somehow recapture the *Queen Mary*, our fate was certain, as we would never be able to reach Shanghai alive, the whole country intervening being full of the ruthless and unscrupulous Imperial soldiery, or, rather, rabble, fighting against the Taiping rebels.

I dismissed the *coolies*, letting them take the game, and then we all walked after them, seeing them a considerable distance on the way back to their village.

Meanwhile, I had come to a determination with my comrades as to our course of action.

Our plan was to strike the river's bank some distance above Kwa-chow, find a boat, then drop silently down with the tide to reconnoitre, and, if possible, retake the *lorcha*. This was, in fact, the only resource we had.

Fortunately, we were all well armed, for, however safe I might think myself, I knew the Chinese character too well, and had had too much experience ever to be off my guard in the way of carrying weapons.

We each had a revolver in addition to our guns, all of which were double-barrels; and, besides this, Ramah had his keen, razor-like *tulwar*—the sharp native sword he had carried as a *sowar* in Fane's horse, whilst Hans had a formidable "bowie," and I wore in my belt a large hunting-knife, fashioned so as to fix on the end of my gun like a bayonet.

When the beautiful Se-she saw us turn off in the direction of the river, she suspected our intention was to try and recapture the vessel, and she clung to me, crying—

"Oh, ngo-te ngae! Puh che! Puh che! Ngo-te foo yau shar ne!" (Oh, my love! Do not go! Do not go! My father will kill you!)

I endeavoured to pacify the poor girl, and tried to induce her to remain in some of the cottages we were passing every now and then, for I dreaded to have her with us during the deadly fight that might, and almost surely would, ensue.

But the devoted darling would not hear of leaving me. She had now left her father—her only relative—she said, and henceforth her lot was mine ; my people should be her people, my home should be her home, and whithersoever I went there would she follow.

What could I do but yield to so much love and devotion ?

It was nearly ten o'clock when we came to the river's bank, and it was some time before we could find a boat. At length, however, we came upon one, and, as luck would have it, found inside the very thing we wanted—a good long coil of light grass rope.

This was even more important than the oars and sail we also found.

Launching the little craft, we all got into her, put out the oars, and were once more afloat.

Then we sat quiet, drifting down with the tide, and in about half an hour faintly discerned the lights of Kwa-chow, just twinkling through the deep darkness of the night.

Fortunately for us, neither moon nor star could be seen, and the night was intensely dark, the heavens being covered with a dense black pall of heavy, lowering clouds.

Bending on the end of the rope to the boat's little grapnel, we tossed it overboard directly the lights became visible, and then slowly slacked away, for we knew that we were very near to where we had left the *lorcha* moored alongside the village *bund*, and expected, every yard we drifted now, to see her.

Perhaps half the line had been paid out, when suddenly, right astern, not twenty yards distant, and almost overhead, I saw the faint glimmer of a light.

I immediately whispered to my comrades to stop slacking away, for I knew that the light must be the *Queen Mary's* masthead lantern, hoisted either to show us the way to the trap prepared by the treacherous natives, or to guard against collision by showing her position to any junk that might be coming down stream.

The crew had cast off from the *bund*, and had then anchored out in the stream. This was all the better for our scheme.

Hauling in the rope, we then weighed our grapnel, made a drag by using the mast and sail, to which we bent the other end of the line, and next tossed it overboard.

We now pulled out into the stream, leaving the drag to drift down between the *lorcha* and the shore; then, when we had got out to a sufficient distance, we rested on our oars, looked to our arms, and also drifted with the current.

In a few moments the light appeared again, broad off on our starboard hand, and, at almost the same instant, we felt the jerk as the rope caught across our vessel's cable. Instantly we let go the grapnel, and slowly veered away, keeping the bight of the line in our hands. By this means we dropped astern of the *lorcha*, and, by using one part or the other of our rope, could either get directly in her wake or well off on her port quarter. We now took the former position, and found ourselves just within sight of the vessel, which we could barely discern as a dim-looking mass, perhaps forty yards right ahead of us.

Carefully loading our guns with a ball and a charge of heavy buck-shot in each barrel, we started on our perilous enterprise.

Slowly and cautiously we now hauled away on that part of the rope caught across the *Queen Mary's* cable, till at length, without being discovered, we were right under her port counter.

Crouching low in the boat, we waited a moment in the most breathless suspense. We could hear the sound of voices, but, where we lay, were safely hidden from the view of those on deck.

Light was streaming from the cabin windows. Slowly raising my head upon a level with the nearest stern port, I peered within.

There they were—the mutineers and their allies—right before my eyes, and only a few feet distant!

There was my money, piled up on the cabin table, with our false *lowder* and the Mandarin busily engaged counting it out and placing it in small divisions, evidently to be shared among the eager crowd of crew and *braves* thronging around them.

I counted the crew. All were there but three or four, and I knew how securely *one* of them had been disposed of. Then I numbered the *braves*. There were eleven of them present, leaving but one to be on deck with the sailors, probably keeping watch for our return.

Now or never was our chance to try and retake the *lorcha*, whilst nearly all her captors were busy gloating over the plunder down below.

A terrible idea struck me, as I surveyed the position. I felt a fierce exultation at thinking how nicely we could trap and destroy nearly the whole of our enemies at one blow!

In cautious whispers I unfolded the plan to my companions. They approved it, and at once we proceeded to put it into execution.

"Here," whispered Hans, "here ist a rope dat ist hanging over der stern."

Placing the blade of my knife between my teeth, and loosening the revolver in my belt, I grasped the rope, and, despite the attempt

made to prevent me by poor Se-she, who was trembling convulsively
with suppressed fear and anguish, slowly hoisted myself up hand over
hand.

I rested for a moment or two, twisting my feet round the rope,
when my head was just below the vessel's taffrail; but then, hearing
nothing, gently raised myself a few inches and gazed on board.

So far as I could see in the dark—and, depend upon it, my sight
was strained to the utmost—there was not a soul on the quarter-deck.
In all probability, those on guard were waiting for us near the
gangway, amidships. I felt pretty well satisfied that, as it was too
dark for me to see any one, it was equally impossible for any one to
see me. Slowly and stealthily I crawled upon the taffrail, then sank
below it to the deck, where I paused again, with a feeling, too, of
mingled wrath and grim merriment at the manner in which I was
compelled to board my own vessel. After listening intently for a few
minutes, I was able to distinguish the muttering of voices somewhere
amidships on deck, as well as the sound of those beneath me in the
cabin.

Creeping up to a locker on the quarter-deck, I took out a couple
of the terrible missiles kept there, and also brought out the iron bar
and padlock of the cabin hatchway.

At this instant the sound of footsteps coming aft alarmed me.
I laid down at full length by the side of the locker and the skylight,
drawing my revolver, cocking it, and taking a firm grip of my long
hunting-knife.

Providentially, the man came up on the other side of the deck,
and so the shelter I had taken advantage of effectually concealed me.
He went down the companion-hatch into the cabin.

Now was my time! Crawling to the hatchway, I softly drew

the slide over it, placed the bar on, and locked it with the padlock, putting the key into my pocket. In another instant I had slid down to my anxious and expectant companions, taking care to carry the terrible *stink-pots* ([1]) with me.

Ramah displayed a truly Indian stoicism, and spoke not a word; but Hans, in spite of his phlegmatic disposition, could not help eagerly asking—

" Vell, mein vriend, how hast doo made out ?"

" All right, old boy! all right!" I replied, in a whisper. " Get your flint and steel; light the joss-stick here on top of these stink-pots. We'll give the wretches a salute through the stern ports that will astonish them!"

" Der tyvel !" cried Dutchy, " dat ist goot ! dat ist goot !"

Then he struck a light, ignited the joss-stick, and I replaced the now burning material on the hollow tops of the missiles, so as to be ready to throw them—the slightest fall being sufficient to break them—when the fire would come into contact with the contents, the whole machine being within a thin bag.

We waited breathlessly a moment, dreading lest the slight noise made by the flint and steel might have betrayed us; but not a sound, save the gentle *lap lap* of the waves against the vessel's sides, with now and then an indistinct murmur from within, could be heard.

We hauled up close to the stern ports, then fixed the boat with a hitch of the rope round the foremost thwart. Snatching up our guns, and taking a steady aim through two of the open ports, we all three fired at the same instant.

([1]) This terrible missile is made of thin clay, filled with a highly combustible compound, which emits the most horrible burning material and suffocating fumes. It is used as a hand-grenade, and is peculiar to Chinese warfare.

Both the *lowder* and the Mandarin fell to our first shots—we had made sure of them; and we poured in the contents of our second barrels before the astonished crowd of Chinamen could tell whence the sudden death was coming amongst them. But when we hurled the fearful hand-grenades upon them they rushed towards the ports with a loud yell, firing off their guns and pistols as they came.

I felt a sharp burning sensation as a bullet whizzed past, abrading the skin of my neck, and heard a slight exclamation of pain from one of my companions; but the next moment, hauling on the grapnel rope, we were out of the line of fire, and away on the *lorcha's* quarter.

"Haul away, boys! Haul away on the drag rope now, and let us get alongside," I cried to my comrades, in an intense undertone.

We tore through the water, were alongside in an instant, and, after making fast to the vessel's main-chains, and leaving Se-she seated in the stern-sheets of the boat, we sprang on board, knife and pistol in hand.

Rushing aft, we found five or six natives tearing at the cabin hatchway, and striving to liberate their stifling friends below, whose shrieks were horrible.

Too late they heard our rush, and turned to meet us; but the sharp and rapid detonations of our revolvers rang echoing through the still night air, and three of their number fell prone and helpless to the deck. Three others, however, sprang upon us; and the next moment I found myself closely engaged with a huge native, who, by his dress, I knew to be the remaining *brave*.

I had fired full at my assailant's breast as he ran towards me, and knew, by the yell he gave, that the shot must have taken effect;

E

but it could not have inflicted any serious injury, as he still rushed on, grappled with me, and cried to his companions—

"Tah! tah! Shar Yang-quitzo!" (Fight! fight! Kill the foreign devils!)

The force with which the fellow sprang upon me threw me down. I lost my knife in the fall, but retained the revolver, and dragged my antagonist with me. Over and over we rolled upon the deck, but neither could use the weapon with which he was armed, for his right hand had a firm grip of my left wrist, whilst my other hand was equally employed upon *his* left, in which he carried a formidable dagger. I soon found that, in spite of his wound, from which the warm blood came trickling over me, my strength was no match for him. Suddenly dropping his weapon, he shook off the grasp of my right hand, then fastened his fingers upon my throat with a grip of iron, from which I found it impossible to release myself. He was strangling me fast! Never shall I forget the terrible agony I endured! Not a breath could I draw; my chest seemed bursting for want of air; my head was even worse, surcharged with blood, racked with pain, and ringing with horrible noises; my eyes felt starting from their sockets. I became insensible.

When consciousness returned, my first sensation was of great pain in the throat; then, by the flickering light of a Chinese lantern, I saw Ramah, Hans, and the blood-stained visage of the "Angel" bending over me. I felt a weight upon my breast, put my hand there, and felt the long silky tresses of Se-she. Then the motion of the vessel told me that she was under weigh, and, glancing aloft, I saw that the sails were set. Just then my foolish old "boy" went down on his knees by my side, blubbering aloud, and crying—

" Oh, Massa Ha-le! mi too mutchee glad you no die. Mi have too mutchee fear you no savey what ting *lowder*, Mandalene, makee do; you come board he makee kille you. Oh, mi just now numbah one too mutchee glad!"

You see, the Chinese are not *all* bad.

The "Angel" is alive, I began to reflect; perhaps my old chum Frank is safe also. With great difficulty I managed to utter his name. My friends gave a mournful shake of the head, and Hans muttered, " Dead! dead!" at the same time pointing to something by my side, and saying, "Thank God, capt'n, you are alive! Der tyvel put I dort dat you vas die!"

Raising myself a little, I gazed where he pointed. There lay poor Frank : hacked and quiet; gashed with many a gory wound; dead and cold.

I was not yet fully sensible, and turned, in a dreamy, stupefied sort of way, to scan the face of her whose head was pillowed in my arms. There was a faint, long-drawn, lingering sigh; the soft lips were raised to mine. I just heard the scarcely-breathed words, " Oh, ngo-te ngae" (Oh, my love!); then the fair young head fell heavily on my breast.

The terrible truth now dawned upon me. Se-she had been wounded in the boat; it was her cry I had heard, but had not noticed in my excitement, and now she had given up her last breath resting in my arms!

I sat up, clasping the inanimate form, and gazed mournfully, helplessly at my friends. I saw in the dim light that even the eyes of the stoical Ramah were wet with tears.

Alas! It was indeed too true; the devoted girl lay a lifeless corpse within my arms. She had saved our lives by sacrificing everything to her love, and coming ashore to warn me, but had perished herself by that cruel shot from the cabin windows—as I found by the red round hole where it had pierced her tender bosom through and through.

Never before did I dream how great an impression the fair young thing had made upon my heart; and now, alas! I had lost her.

What needs it to tell of my bitter grief, my unavailing regret? I have told how she died; a whole language cannot make a more mournful tale of love, sorrow, and devotion. And I had lost my strange, wild love for ever!

When once more I stood upon the deck of my vessel my surviving friends told me how that the murderers had all been stifled by the fumes of the terrible *stink-pots*, save these, indeed, who had sprung overboard from the stern ports in time to escape the frightful death of their friends who perished by burning and suffocation. Some seven or eight of the crew had clambered on board from the water; but all the mutiny had been taken out of them, and they assisted in getting the *lorcha* under-weigh, for it was advisable to get clear of Kwa-chow as soon as possible. When they went to get the unfortunate Se-she out of the boat they found her helpless, fainting, and smothered with blood from the deadly wound in her bosom. They carefully carried her on deck, placing her by my side, for they thought that I, too, was mortally wounded, seeing that I was insensible, and also covered with gore, which, however, had flowed from the *brave* who had attacked me, and whom they had disposed of after having rid themselves of their own assailants. The "Angel" had suddenly made his appearance when they were masters of the deck; he had been wounded during the mutiny of the crew, and he led them to the hold, where, stretched out on the ballast, they found the body of my hapless partner.

THE LAST RESTING-PLACE OF FRANK AND SE-SHE.

Poor Frank! His death was terribly avenged. Never shall I forget the horrible sight that met our gaze when we opened the hatch and proceeded to clear the cabin! Four or five had been killed by our fire; the rest of the miserable wretches had been burnt, suffocated, scorched to death.

The "Angel" declared that the mutiny took place exactly at *six o'clock.*

Dropping down the river as far as the Pawn-pien-shan reach, on our way back to Shanghai, we bore the bodies of my unfortunate friend, and the lovely but ill-fated Se-she to the foot of the great Split-Hill on the northern shore, where the land was clothed with primeval forest; and there, beneath the shade of the drooping cypress boughs, ever waving, mournful, and solemn above their lonely resting-place—at the foot of the ancient, time-worn, monumental sculpture of the grey Yang-shan pagoda—we laid them side by side; the tawny maiden of the East and the pale-faced stranger from afar.

THE LOG.

January 8th.

Seven bells, half-past eleven p.m.—Esmond had just finished his tale, and we were all pretty silent for some few moments. No doubt each thought of poor Se-she, and wondered whether a similar violent death would terminate his own career in that distant land, so fatal to Europeans, with its pirates, its robbers, and its general lawlessness.

Midnight.—The "Angel" (Esmond's steward) appeared to lay the supper, and we all seemed to feel an interest in him, such as we had not known before, as we gazed at the large disfiguring scars upon his face and arms.

A glance of intelligence passed between the "Angel" and his master at the memories revived; then we went to work at our supper.

January 9th.

During all the small hours of this morning, till aroused by the smooth accents and gliding step of that sleek, grave-faced Assam, bringing me the usual cup of steaming hot coffee and plate of buttered toast, I dream of nothing but the bleeding form of poor Se-she, lying still and cold beneath the shade of the mournful waving cypress boughs, and gleaming white monumental sculpture of the tall Yang-chan pagoda.

CHA-PU BAY.

As a ship's harbour log is seldom very interesting—much less when kept upon a mud-bank—we will, in future, omit the ordinary details of the day, and deal only with matters more immediately concerning ourselves, our amusements, and the tales of the respective evenings.

Nothing noteworthy transpired during this day. The schooner remained comfortably embedded in the mud, and we all paid a visit to the neighbouring shore, rambling along the wild, romantic, and picturesque coast-line into which it was broken, whilst I made the accompanying sketch of a spot that I particularly admired, called Cha-pu Bay by the natives.

As eight bells strike we again assemble round the cheering stove, that night, ready for our friend the merchant's yarn.

Whilst the rest of us were mixing our grog, lighting our weeds, and making ourselves generally comfortable, Mr. Lawrence took the chair, and said—

"Well, gentlemen, there is but one story of which I can think, and of this I am myself the hero, so that I shall follow the example of our worthy friend and host, by telling a tale in which the teller is himself personally interested."

"Hear, hear!" roared Jack Backstay, in a voice that seemed to shake the stanch *Fortuna's* very timbers.

We were all pleased with the story-teller's statement, and anxious for him to begin, as we had been fearing that our tales would have too strong a flavour of salt water and the tar-bucket.

"Gentlemen," continued Mr. Lawrence, "you have all met my wife ; I believe one or two of you have heard that our first meeting was strange and romantic.   It was, indeed, very much so!   It is this that I shall now have the pleasure of narrating to you."

Settling himself comfortably in the easiest easy-chair, and lighting a huge "hubble-bubble," at which he vigorously puffed away at every pause, our friend began his tale.

The Merchant's Yarn.

LE PONT NEUF.

A TALE OF PARIS.

DISMAL and dreary appeared the long streets of the French metropolis. The cold wind came sweeping wildly along the deserted thoroughfares, seeming to howl with delight at its undisputed supremacy. The rain and sleet beat heavily in torrents against the closed windows; making the people within gaze complacently on their own shadows as they were brought into fantastic life at the will of the glowing embers, each flash of which created strange gigantic bodies and huge contorted members. So very empty were the endless streets, that the lamps seemed lighting a lost city—an interminable desert of brickwork, forsaken by all things that had the breath of life. Had it not been that something of modern existence could now and then be seen, the solitude would have been oppressive; fortunately, at rare intervals, some solitary *gendarme* would come into view, though, whenever the muffled-up figure of cocked hat, cape, and boots, came into sight, it evinced a very decided preference for large porticoes or deep doorways, and soon became invisible again beneath the friendly shelter of some dark archway. Passengers were rare, and though the hour was comparatively early, the streets of the gay city were almost deserted; but then it was a wretched night, and none but the belated traveller, or those whose avocations kept them out late, were likely to be away from home.

As I strode along homeward, puffing fiercely at my cigar, I

began to regret that I had not accepted my friend Victor D'Orsay's invitation to pass the night at his comfortable chambers ; however, in the sequel I found reason to rejoice at my determination.

Having once lived long in Paris, I had many friends there, but on this occasion was only making a short stay *en passant*, on my return to England from the East Indies.

Well, I felt savage and miserable, trudging along those muddy streets of the oldest part of the Faubourg St. Germain ; but I met with an adventure that night—an adventure which not only made me acquainted with an atrocious system of crime, but had the result of making me happy for life. I succeeded in baulking a couple of murderers, saving the life of their intended victim, bringing the criminals to justice, and obtaining a dear little wife for myself. Rather a good night's work, I flatter myself. Thank heaven I did not accept Victor's urgent solicitation!

I had to cross the Seine, in order to reach my hotel near the Tuileries, and I made for the nearest bridge—Le Pont Neuf.

Upon entering a dark street that led to the bank of the river, I came in sight of a female form hastening forward in the same direction. Dark as it was, we were yet near enough for me to see that the stranger was well dressed ; young I felt assured she must be, by her gracefulness of form and lightness of step.

My interest was at once awakened. Who could she be, out on this tempestuous night ? Bound, too, for that evilly-reputed Pont Neuf!

This ill-omened structure, I at once reflected, was—taking a metaphysical view of it - the counterpart of our Waterloo Bridge. Both are affected by suicides. Who ever heard of any one taking their last dive from Blackfriars, or any other than the favoured bridge ? Who ever knew of the Parisian plunging from anywhere but Le Pont Neuf? It is a strange—a ghastly fact; but no less indisputable than inexplicable. Why go they there, these *misérables?* Why always to the same spot, when anywhere would equally well serve their wretched purpose? We are the slaves of fashion; perhaps that explains it. Our belles make small waists and wear chignons, because they are fashionable; the Chinese women cripple their feet because others do so; those who are tired of life in London and Paris, and choose ending it by water, rush to the one or the other of the aforesaid bridges, because they know that many have gone there before them, and because, when thinking for the fatal place, Le Pont Neuf or Waterloo Bridge most likely makes the first impression on their distempered brain.

Such fancies as these affected me, and I walked faster, so as to overtake the strange female before she should reach the bridge. I came up with her just as we both passed on to it. One glance was sufficient. She was no suicide. The gaslight was strong enough just there to show me that her eyes were clear and calm; no suicidal mania shone in their full bright depths; but a very angry flash came into them at my earnest gaze, and a thick veil was quickly lowered before a sweet little face that I at once perceived was extremely beautiful. I had just time to notice the small regular features, the profusion of rich chestnut tresses, and the glittering large eyes, when they were effectually hidden from me. This mysterious girl, who came wandering to that fatal bridge so late at night—alone, too, in the dark and storm—was well, though plainly dressed, and her slender figure, barely of the medium height, I could yet see, in spite of the muffling cloak, was strikingly graceful, and of a charmingly developed contour.

I could not resist the temptation. In my best French—and that must, I fear, have sounded rather barbarous to ears Parisian —I politely asked permission to escort her over the bridge.

"Non, merci, Monsieur," was the only reply vouchsafed.

The fair stranger's manner was so full of natural dignity and maidenly reserve, that I could not do more than raise my hat and walk on. It was obviously quite impossible to repeat my request, and I went my way wondering.

Upon passing the statue in the centre of the bridge I looked back and saw her following, perhaps thirty yards behind, for I could only just discern her through the storm and darkness.

I had gone but little further, when I was suddenly startled by a wild cry for help.

I knew it to be her voice; besides, that fearful scream came from the very spot which she could just have reached.

I rushed back, a loud splash in the water making me fear the worst.

At the same moment two men ran swiftly past me. They came from the direction whence the shriek had come; and, as they were separating, I plainly heard one say to the other—

"À minuit—par le Maison Rouge!"

What meant this strange expression? "At midnight—by the Red House!"

I had not time to consider it then, neither to pursue the fugitives, for the young girl had disappeared from the bridge. However, just as the two men were passing me, I picked up a good-sized stone, and as they would not obey my summons to halt, hurled it with all my force at the tallest. At this instant he glanced over his shoulder, and I knew that the missile must have taken effect on the side of his face, for he threw up his hands to it, and staggered almost to falling. This little episode, together with the exclamation already noticed, did good service by-and-by. All this happened within a minute from the outcry, and, as I reached the centre of the bridge, and gazed earnestly upon the murky river, running sluggishly below, I suddenly perceived a faint white rippling, from whence came another cry—half smothered this time—for help.

Thank heaven! I was an expert swimmer, and the bridge was not more than fifteen or twenty feet above the water. Throwing off my upper garments, and kicking off my boots, I sprang forward with all my strength, taking a dive that brought me up just where I desired—right in the centre of the circling white ripples. In a moment I felt the drowning grasp upon me. The darkness over that inky river was so great that I could not see who held me, but I felt the face, touched the luxuriant hair now tangled in the water, and knew that it was the young girl I had before addressed.

I tried to free myself, to hold her so that I could swim. To my horror, however, she clung to me so tightly, and with such rigidness, that I could not even manage to keep afloat.

Down we went! Down, down, deeper yet, till I felt the slimy black ooze at the bottom of the river.

The sinking did not trouble me, for I could have held my breath much longer; but I shuddered at the thought that we might perhaps stick fast in that horrid mud and slime, there to mingle with the loathsome objects held already, and keep company with other dead, drowned things.

Soft, pulpy substances were swept against us; long dank leaves of sedgy plants kept clutching and twining around us, ready—too ready—to welcome us down to their dark and watery abode. We were swept against one of these unseen clusters of aquatic vegetation, which threw such strong and wiry tendrils about us as made me fear that it would hold us for ever. With a great effort I broke away, and we then rose slowly up to the surface.

A moment to breathe! to see the lowering black clouds hanging as a funeral pall above us, whilst the rain, like pitying tear-drops, came heavily down from its dense, watery fountains, and fell plashing around us with a melancholy sound; to see the sombre opaqueness of the frowning heavens, joining the still blacker line of the distant city, so oblivious of our danger, so heedless of our dying struggles, as we swept helpless along that dark and dismal river! A moment to see all this; to appreciate the utter hopelessness of our situation; to feel the bitter disappointment of failing to attract the attention of those who could save us on board yonder bark, looming vast, strange, and ghost-like through the murky air, and past which we quickly glide; then down again to the inky water's eager embrace.

We were under water so long this time that it nearly exhausted me.

I began to get delirious, and fancy, though my eyes were closed, that I could see all that river's horrible tenancy about us: the glistening white bones of those who had perished long ago as we were doing—the loathsome, creeping, crawling things that live in foul waters and feed upon the dead—the frightful bloated bodies of the lately drowned—all hideous things seemed eagerly thronging around us in a ghastly sort of merriment. Added to these pleasant fancies was the agonising sensation of suffocation.

Once more, thank God! we rose to the surface; rose, too, just as I could feel those slender yet firm limbs relaxing and untwining from about me.

"WE DRIFTED ON."

Getting my right arm free, I felt at ease in the water; and then, after resting awhile, proceeded to turn my insensible burden, after which I pulled her close to me, placed both her hands under my chin, and clasped them there. She was now face up and out of the water, and with her back to mine, in the easiest possible position. If it had not been for the former struggling and exhaustion consequent upon twice sinking with her, I could have carried her like this for miles, for I was at home in the water. As it was, I knew that my strength would not last much longer, and so endeavoured to reserve it by merely drifting with the current, instead of exhausting myself by striking out for the distant bank. Moreover, I had heard that the tide set direct from the Pont Neuf to a part of the shore some two or three miles distant, where the river took a sharp bend to the eastward. I had also heard that to this spot usually floated the poor remains of those who had madly quitted the cares and sorrows of life by taking the fatal plunge into the cool, obliterating waters; so I made myself easy, and went the same way. But I doubt whether any who had gone before ever afterwards described the journey.

Time flew by, and we drifted on, but were so little nearer to the shore that I half began to fear we might never again reach it alive.

I was getting very tired and very cold.

My thoughts took a gloomy turn, and, in fancy, I saw us lying side by side upon some quiet strand, appealing so mutely, so pitifully, to those who came down wonderingly to view us, for some few feet of their land whereon to rest our finished frames and hide them from the world.

But then, suppose we did not touch the shore!

F 2

Suppose we were drifted out into the wide, wide sea!

I thought of the monsters of the deep, and shuddered even more than I shivered with the cold. I thought of Victor Hugo and his devil-fish; thought, too, that as we were drifting out towards the French coast we might fall into the clutches of the very one that he had seen—if he did see one. I trusted, however, that his strange monster was imaginary; but I remembered ugly stories tending to confirm the truth of the existence of such, though what all this mattered when we should be dead I could not at the time perceive. Yet I could not leave the subject; it seemed to possess a strange fascination, and, after all, we were not so far from putting these dismal conjectures to the test. If we escaped the monstrous sea-things, it would only be to float unburied on the deep, to startle, mayhap, in the grey of coming night, the mariner of some passing ship, who, from high mast-head, would turn sick and fearful at the sight of the two upturned white faces gleaming fitfully in the uncertain light, and who would wonder, with a shudder, whether *his* body, too, might not some day beat unburied over the remorseless seas, and then perhaps, would form a prayer for his rest—his long last rest—in some quiet green churchyard of the inland home that had almost been forgotten. Then I began to think of that fierce and swiftly-gliding monster; that unquiet demon of the deep—the ravenous shark! But even as my wandering fancy took this turn, some hard substance struck against me, and, I fear, a loud cry escaped me as I thought that the terrible jaws of six-rowed jagged teeth were closing upon us.

How great, however, was my delight! How great the revulsion of feeling!

It was land—or, rather, mud—at last!

Whilst dreaming as described, I had failed to notice that we were being drifted to the bank. Splashing and falling through shallow water, slime, and sedge, I fell with my burden upon dry land. How fervently I thanked the good God for guiding us to this spot! For, had the bank been steep, I should never, in my exhausted and encumbered state, have been able to get ashore. Upon recovering my strength a little, I unloosed the handkerchief with which I had bound the fair stranger's hands around my neck; then tenderly placed her in the most comfortable position, and strove to reanimate her; but without success, for she remained unconscious, in spite of my efforts. Then I started up in quest of assistance.

What was my astonishment—I might almost say horror—to find that the nearest house, only some fifty yards from the river's bank, was of a deep *red* colour! It at once struck me as being the Maison Rouge of the assassins. Dark stories I had heard of doings on the river Seine, now recurred to my mind; but I was quickly recalled to the necessity of prompt action, by hearing the church bells strike half-past eleven, and remembering that the tall man had appointed midnight as the time for what I now imagined meant their meeting on this very spot. Running back to where I had left my insensible charge, I lifted her in my arms and carried her to the door of the first house beyond the red one. Everybody had gone to bed, and it was some moments ere any reply was obtained in answer to my loud and repeated knocking. At length, however, a huge, white-cotton-night-capped head was thrust out of an upper window, and the owner thereof angrily cried—

"Que du diable me voulez vous?"

In as few words as possible I told him my adventure, and begged that he would at once come down and take charge of the poor girl, who, I feared, was dying, whilst I ran for a doctor. Fortunately, we had fallen in with a good Samaritan.

"Jour de ma vie!" I heard him exclaim, as he left the window, and proceeded to shout in so vigorous a manner that the whole household was soon aroused and thronging round us.

Leaving my charge in the hands of the worthy citizen and his dame, I flew to the corner of the street, where a doctor resided, whom I brought back with me. I rejoiced, however, to find that his attentions were almost needless, the warmth and stimulants that the good people were applying having already restored the beautiful girl to consciousness. The moment I entered the room she saw me, and, starting half up from the bed, her low exclamations of gratitude, the faintly-struggling blush upon her pale cheeks, and the eloquent glances of her large and deep-blue eyes were not without effect, wet, faint, and uncomfortable as I was.

By this time—especially as the storm had passed over and the night turned fine—some *gendarmes* became visible. It was the revolutionary period, and these guardians of the public peace were armed to the teeth, with musket, bayonet, sword, and pistol. To make up for lost time, they were amusing themselves by shouting the time of night with perfectly frantic vehemence, accompanied with the pleasing information (to all who might hear it) that the weather had turned fine. Speaking to a couple, and telling them my suspicions, they readily accompanied me to the river's bank, where we lay in wait, close to the Maison Rouge, for those I expected.

I was clad in a dry rig-out of the hospitable citizen's clothes, which I had put on anyhow in my hurry—the appointed hour having almost arrived—and I had just gathered tight under my belt the last of the superabundant folds, when we heard the echoing sound of the

THE GENDARMES.

midnight chimes come booming sonorously from the great bell in the
lofty tower of Notre Dame.

We were just in the outskirt of the Faubourg St. Germain, and
the striking of the myriad church clocks—from the deep, full, and
richly-toned bell of the cathedral, through every variety of musical
metallic clang, to the insignificant tinkle in the smallest chapel belfry—
came rolling through the still night air with exceeding pleasant and
impressive effect.

The Maison Rouge, under the walls of which we were hiding,
stood some little distance from the end of the last street, and nearer
to the water.

The booming reverberation, after being taken up from point to
point, and repeated from church to church, was just dying away in the
distance, when the noise of approaching footsteps placed us on the alert.

Though the night was now fine, it was yet very dark, and I
could not at first recognise the approaching figures. But when they
passed within a few yards of the shaded corner where we were
hidden I knew them instantly : my suspicions had proved correct ;
they were the two men of the Pont Neuf! I whispered so to my
companions ; whereat one of them—a corporal, upon whom, in con-
sideration of his official rank, the command of the detachment had
devolved—lugged forth a note-book, and made some entries in the
dark, chuckling to himself, and several times repeating, "Aha !
Messieurs les Assassins. C'est bon ! c'est bon !"—after having
solemnly asked me whether I was positive as to their identity, and
then told his comrade to attest my evidence. No doubt the corporal
was looking forward to distinguish himself in a *cause célèbre*.

Whispering to us that we must play the *mouchard* for a few
moments, our commander led us stealthily after the two murderous

wretches. They had just stepped over the river's bank, and got down on the narrow muddy beach, so we crawled close up to the edge, and then laid down to listen.

We had not long to wait.

With brutal oaths, the ruffians were wondering how it was that the body had not yet drifted to the spot; we heard enough, moreover to connect them with many another case—cases of *successful* murder. After peering over the dark surface of the river a little longer, and muttering many a horrid curse at the delay, they sat down to wait, and lighted their pipes, within a couple of yards of where we lay.

The moment for action had now arrived. The wretches were sitting with their backs turned our way. Silently raising ourselves erect, we sprang upon them. They were secured in a moment.

We had nothing like one of your London street-fights with the police, where any ruffian can resist being arrested, and the policeman can only meet him upon almost equal terms in a pugilistic encounter. Nothing of the sort here. In Paris the *gendarmes* have very little difficulty about securing a prisoner; they are all armed, and the delinquent is well aware that he *must* submit, or, perhaps, be killed.

Both my companions had drawn their swords, flourishing them with one hand, whilst each held one of our prisoners with the other. The murderers were so surprised by our sudden attack, and, probably, so awed by the flash of the steel, that they made not the slightest attempt at resistance. They did not even rise to their feet till the corporal ordered them to get up, so as to enable us to secure them with the handcuffs he had given me to hold.

Previous to taking them before the Commissaire of Police, we led our prisoners into the presence of their intended victim, who unhesitatingly identified them as the men who had thrown her over the bridge; and she further deposed that they had rushed upon her from behind the equestrian statue on its centre, where they had been lying in concealment.

The ruffians began to appear ill at ease. Evidence was accumulating against them pretty fast.

The only thing that seemed difficult to ascertain was the motive for their crime—the lady declaring that they were perfect strangers to her. However, I had already formed my own opinion of the matter, and the theory proved quite correct.

Before leaving the room, I noticed, among other articles spread out to dry, the cards that had been taken from the pocket of her I had so fortunately saved. Slyly stealing one of these, directly I got outside the door I hastily perused it by the light of the lamp on the staircase—

> MDLLE. ADÈLE DE BIRON,
>
> *Professeur de Musique et de Chant.*

So ran the card. And thus was accounted for the lateness of the hour at which its fair owner was abroad. No doubt, poor girl! she had many a long tramp in the wet and dark, without much of profit or pleasure, for the governess is almost worse paid in Paris than in London, and some of the pupils are quite as thick-headed.

When we reached his abode, and managed to rouse him out, the Commissaire at once committed our prisoners to the Préfecture, upon the strength of our depositions; though, I am half inclined to fancy, it would have taken even considerably less evidence to produce the same result: for he seemed mightily wroth at being disturbed, and appeared perfectly ready to visit upon any unfortunate victim the full weight of his virtuous indignation.

Of course, the moment that the prisoners were safely lodged I went back to where I had left the beautiful Adèle. Finding her sufficiently recovered, as well as terribly anxious to proceed home, I had the pleasure of taking her there in a *fiacre*. After what had passed, it may easily be imagined that we became great friends before reaching her abode. I found that she lived alone with her widowed mother, whom she supported by teaching music and singing. Mentally, I at once declared that the rising generation of Paris should soon be obliged to get some one else to teach them accomplishments.

The poor mother was sitting up for her daughter in extreme anxiety and alarm—for it was now past two o'clock in the morning. Never shall I forget the terror she exhibited on hearing of her child's peril, and her intense gratitude when told of how I chanced to be of service.

Well, the beautiful Adèle never again walked home alone and unprotected so late at night, after giving a long and tedious hour's instruction to some wretched *enfant* for two or three *francs*.

I became a constant visitor at that quiet little home. Often, as we paused together on the Pont Neuf, and, hand in hand, from the very spot whence we had taken our giddy flight that night, gazed down upon the dark waters, flowing on as placidly as ever, we interchanged the words of love and hope. By the time that the trial came on I occupied the proud position of the lovely Adèle's accepted suitor. It is sometimes a good thing to be a first-rate swimmer.

Many had missed some unfortunate relative whom the ruthless waters of the Seine had discovered, and the unhappy friends of some so found had solemnly declared their conviction that murder, not suicide, had been perpetrated; the strangest thing being that no

ADÈLE.

motive for assassination could be anywhere assigned, neither any one
discovered upon whom suspicion could alight.   Dark rumours, in
consequence, had gradually arisen.   Thus it came to pass that the

Palàis de Justice was thronged in every part on the morning fixed for the trial of Adéle's assailants.

The two prisoners were arraigned; and villanous-looking scoundrels they were in the clear light of the day. The tallest, a huge, brawny ruffian, with cunning, cruel little black eyes, and a short stubbly beard spreading unshaved all over his bloated face; the other, a short, thick-set idiot, evidently the tool and slave of the former; his gaunt, expressionless countenance showing nothing more distinctive than a huge mouth, great, beardless, heavy jaws, and a pair of large, light-coloured, vacant eyes, that contained no trace of other intelligence than, perhaps, a lurking indication of dull, apathetic ferocity.

THE ASSASSINS.

The most breathless interest prevailed throughout the court; and at every pause in the proceedings, the fall of the proverbial pin might easily have been heard.

The evidence was terribly conclusive, and, as fact after fact accumulated against them, the air of bravado assumed by the biggest ruffian gradually subsided into very visible symptoms of fear and uneasiness.

I proved having seen them running from the spot where Adéle was thrown over the bridge, and at the very moment I heard her fall into the water. Then mentioned that I had thrown a stone at the tallest, striking him on the left side of the face—the scar was there, on his left cheek, and hardly yet quite healed. Next I swore to his exclamation—" A minuit—par le Maison Rouge!" and proved that that was where we drifted, and where they came at the appointed hour to find *one* of us; little dreaming, I suppose, that the man who passed them on the bridge had discovered their murderous attempt, and been so fortunate as to save the intended victim. Then, together with the two *gendarmes*, I described the conversation we had over-heard whilst the ruffians were sitting waiting for the supposed corpse to float ashore. Adèle's evidence effectually confirmed the case against the prisoners at the bar, whom she recognised as the men that had rushed upon her from behind the statue of Henri Quatre, in the middle of the bridge, and who had then lifted her up and thrown her into the river.

At this stage of the proceedings the leading savage turned crown evidence in the hope of saving himself. Even this seemed incapable of exciting his idiotic companion, who merely gave a curse, and then relapsed into his old state of careless indifference. From beginning to end the monster confessed the whole horrible story of how, in order to obtain the paltry reward given by the authorities to those who took dead bodies from the Seine and carried them to the Morgue, he and his companion had for years been in the habit of increasing the number by laying in wait for any weak and unwary passenger, and tossing the poor unfortunate over the Pont Neuf, knowing that from there the body would drift ashore near the Maison Rouge.

Fortunately for justice (though the wretch had confessed, and it was impossible to bring directly home to either of them any particu-lar case of murder), although these atrocious criminals escaped with their lives, it is, at least, doubtful whether penal servitude for life—the sentence they received—is not a greater punishment.

Paris was edified, justice appeased, and Adèle is my wife; and so ends this authentic narrative concerning Le Pont Neuf.

THE LOG.

Midnight.—We were all acquainted with the charming Adéle, and it may easily be imagined what a tempest of congratulations greeted the conclusion of the merchant's yarn. Many a man would be only too glad to risk his life for the chance of obtaining so beauteous and accomplished a bride as the fair partner of our friend Lawrence ; lucky dog that he was!—though *I* cannot complain, as will be seen by-and-by. Nevertheless, he was exceedingly lucky, for nothing but most unusual swimming qualities could possibly have saved either of their lives, and here is where he had the luck—those qualities were his. Many people may feel inclined to doubt the possibility of such a swim in, and escape from, the Seine, but then they have not known the gentleman to whom the adventure occurred, or their doubts would cease. *We*, knowing his aquatic powers, nothing doubted. In fact, supply him with provisions, and I verily believe that he could swim from London to New York.

"Ah!" sighed Esmond, "happy fellow—happy fellow, Lawrence! I wish that I had such a wife."

Then my poor old chum, mechanically as it were, lighted a fresh manilla, and sank back in his chair with a painful, strained expression fixed upon his handsome features. Poor fellow! He envied our happy friend. Perhaps he thought of the unfortunate Se-she, and regretted the fair young thing that sacrificed her life in saving his.

What with the conversation, inquiries, and reveries produced by the merchant's story, time flew by unheeded on the wing, and Esmond forgot to call the "Angel" and order supper, till at last *ting ting* went the bell, and Jack Backstay, starting from the brown study into which he had fallen, electrified us all by the formidable tones in which he shouted—

"By the hump on the back of Mahomet's big camel—and that was as big as the Rock of Gibraltar—there's two bells (one o'clock a.m.) striking!"

Just then the "Angel" intruded his expansive physiognomy round the corner of the pantry, and, addressing Esmond, said—

"Master, one o'clock have makee : more bettah mi puttee supper ?"

"Ah—can do, can do," cried our skipper, waking up and rousing himself with an effort from the long and sorrowful reverie upon which the loud-voiced Jack had broken.

January 10th.

As the evening of this day displayed a decided attachment to the cold and rain that had prevailed since sunrise, we mustered around the cuddy stove at an earlier hour than usual, and spent the interval before eight bells in talking and yarning upon various matters ; amongst others, the subject of ghosts became broached. The doctor was a very firm believer in these supernatural gentry, but every one else, except Jack Backstay, laughed at him. That sturdy mariner, however, seemed seriously impressed with the subject, and, like the sailor's parrot, although he did not talk much, was, no doubt, a deuce of a fellow to think. This set me scheming, as it was my turn to tell the first of the tales I had promised, and I had not yet formed the most remote idea of what my yarn was to be about. But now ghosts got into my head, and I determined to give both Jack and the doctor a dose.

Precisely as eight bells struck I astonished my ready audience by informing them that I intended to give them a ghost story—the more so, no doubt, as I had wisely observed a discreet reticence during the late argument.

Dr. O'Kilorkure sprang up from his seat, overjoyed at finding, as he thought, another supporter of his faith in the spirit world. In the excitement of the moment his brogue came out pretty strong, as he cried—

"Ah, thin, I tould ye so! Bravo, me boy, bravo! It's yerself that 'ill know how to prove the thruth that ghosts exist. Sure now, me boys, what 'ill ye have to say to the three of us, eh? The majority carries the day, to be sure it does! Hooroo! Fire away! Go ahead, me boy!"

Upon receiving this conjurgation, I began my yarn at once. It is an old story that I heard at sea years ago.

THE GHOST ON BOARD THE "IMOGENE."

A LEGEND OF THE SEA.

All, my friends, I fancy you will exclaim, when you hear the title of my story, "not a very pleasant thing that." A ghost on board ship! Yes, most assuredly such a visitation *is* unpleasant; in fact, we may venture to affirm, without fear of contradiction, that it is decidedly unwelcome and terrible.

Now, long-shore folk are sometimes troubled with visitors—or, what is almost as satisfactory, imagine that they are—from the other world. When this is the case—when dreadful and sanguinary murder is supposed to have been committed within the haunted walls; when one of the former inmates of the house is supposed to have died in a strange, mysterious manner, and ever afterwards to make uneasy manifestations of spirit (indeed, in such cases there is generally a superabundance of spirits)—when these things happen, all that has to be done is to pack up and move to the next street or so.

Doors may creak and shake during the stilly hours of the night, as though invisible forms were passing in and out, but not forgetting to make a noise to jar one's nerves. Strange, inexplicable sounds may be heard reverberating throughout the dull, old-fashioned house. The forms of anciently-murdered, frilled, faded, and furbelowed ladies are seen gliding about, as the straggling moonbeams play through the diamond panes, and dance fantastically along the old and dusty corridors. A rustling silken dress and a pointing hand generally finish up this picture, with, perhaps, a sad, mournful expression of its ghastly countenance, if the narrator has been fortunate enough to see the spectral features of outraged and unavenged innocence; or the presence is described as having vanished into thin air, with a low wail of agony, &c., if the ghost beholder happened to hear more than he or she could see. Yet, no matter how hysterical or superstitious a person may be, these things can always be avoided on *terra firma*, for there is plenty of room. The haunted places may be left hundreds of miles behind, and the individual troubled by such unearthly appearances can cut and run. But how is a ghost to be dodged if it takes up its unearthly quarters on board ship?

You cannot give warning and quit the premises if you are of a temper which prefers peace to parley, and which ghosts agitate; neither can you have the melancholy satisfaction of calling in Policeman X if you should happen to be of a stubborn disposition—a sort of person who likes to fight things out, especially with the majesty of the law on the right side, even when they are positively mysterious, if not supernatural. If you are ever so pugnaciously inclined, you cannot take a bottle of brandy, a brace of six-chambered revolver rifles, and a plucky friend, wherewith to make a night of it by the side of a blazing fire, and settle the ghost, because, on board such a ship as the *Imogene*, there are no more cats than catch mice; neither bottles of brandy nor sacks of coal to be obtained from the next shop, nor friends plucky enough to waste their watch below in looking for *impalpable* spirits when they are pretty well occupied with the duties of watch and watch.

Cooped within the narrow limits of a six hundred ton ship, the land hundreds of miles away, a waste of waters all around, and nothing but a few frail planks between life and eternity, it is not difficult to imagine the terrible situation of those doomed to a long, wearisome, monotonous voyage, with some supernatural presence to make their isolated little home quite hideous.

People may talk as they please about the increase of civilisation and the decrease of ignorant superstition, but, nevertheless, the fact that their neighbours are just as full as ever with mysterious occurrences and ghost stories remains patent.

On the 9th day of September, 18—, the good ship *Imogene* left the London Docks, bound to Bombay, E.I. Captain Grey, her commander, was one of the best seamen and smartest young skippers sailing out of England. Her crew, all told, numbered twenty-three persons. When the ship's articles were signed, the shipping master had said—

"Well, captain, I think you have as fine a crew as ever trod plank, or left this office; but I must say I don't exactly like the look of that last hand."

"What, the man I picked up in place of the one that was taken ill and could not sign?" the captain said.

"Ay, that's the fellow. 'A Rhode Island horse,' I heard him 'kalkerlating' he was, as he left the office, disputing about the time to get his traps aboard."

"Ah, Mr. Shippem, the man cannot help his looks," said Captain Grey. "His characters are all 'very good.'"

"Well, sir, he *may* be a good man, but I certainly don't like 'the cut of his jib;' but it is your affair, and, as you have taken him as sailmaker, you'll have many opportunities to study his physiognomy when he's patching up your 'flying kites' on the poop—a work that,

ELI BOGGS.

by all accounts, he will get in plenty, for you have a regular reputation as a 'carrying on' skipper."

And so the subject dropped.

Eli Boggs, of Rhode Island, U.S. of America, got on board with the rest of the crew, duly drunk and helpless, the moment before she cast off from the Dock Heads and had the end of a steam-tug's tow-rope hitched round her forecastle bitts.

Nothing worthy of notice took place until the *Imogene* had crossed the Line. Although Captain Grey had not yet found reason to repent his choice of a sailmaker, he had seen enough to convince him that that individual was really a disagreeable and dangerous character, in spite of the "very goods" inscribed on his certificates. No particular act had caused this belief—in fact, the captain would have been puzzled to give any satisfactory reason for it; but many little things, and a certain strangeness about the man, seemed to make him generally disliked on board.

The personal appearance of Eli Boggs was unequivocally dead against him. Bony, gaunt, and lank were his proportions. Long, straight, and limp was the hair about his head and face. His eyes were stony, hollow, and immovable—as one might imagine the eyes of a dead serpent, only they seemed, somehow, like the slight covering of a hidden volcano. Silent, morose, and vindictive he certainly was : just the sort of man a slight offence would make a deadly enemy.

Eli Boggs had a very Yankee and unpleasant habit of squirting over the decks huge jets of tobacco-juice that always filled his mouth. He had frequently been taken to task by the officers, but as he did not heed their orders, they at last complained to their superior.

Captain Grey was by no means harsh or tyrannical with his men ; he happily combined the *suaviter in modo* with the *fortiter in re,* and withal had a way that was easily understood to mean that there was not the slightest compulsion, only you *must* obey. When the sailmaker was hauled up before the " old man " (as sailors say), he fully experienced this sentiment, and as—according to another inveterate habit—he listened to the censure with his head bent down, his chin almost touching his chest, whilst gazing stonily forth beneath his bent brows, his appearance was remarkably sinister and forbidding.

The steward had, somehow, been mixed up in this affair. Either the sailmaker had squirted his tobacco-juice over some clean mats that the former had put out to dry, or he had stained some canvas covers belonging to the cabin ; at all events, the steward was

instrumental in getting his allowance of grog stopped, and though
Eli Boggs said nothing, yet his yellow-mottled, cadaverous face
ever afterwards seemed to turn quite green with suppressed passion
when that individual approached him.

Some weeks had elapsed, and the ship, having caught the
welcome "sou'-west trades," was dashing through the water at the
rate of eight or nine knots an hour, with the starboard main tack
clewed up, and stun'-sails alow and aloft on the same side, when the
vengeance that Eli Boggs cherished against the steward burst
forth.

The captain and officers were down below at dinner, having left
the boatswain in charge of the deck (as is usual in such steady winds
and fine weather). Eli Boggs was working at an old foretopsail,
spread out on the poop. While shifting this sail as he worked, part
of it became drawn over the cabin skylight. Immediately afterwards
the steward came running up on deck, and began hauling away at
the canvas which darkened the dinner-table below. Unfortunately,
whilst so engaged, and as he was vexed at being interrupted in his
duties in the cabin, probably more violent than was necessary, he
managed to drag part of the topsail out of the sailmaker's hands,
at the same time jerking away the latter's sail-hook, and catching
him by the leg with it.

No sooner did Eli Boggs feel the instrument tearing his flesh,
than he sprang from his bench, pulled the hook from his bleeding leg,
and rushed savagely upon the offender. In a moment the steward
was overpowered and struck senseless to the deck. Not satisfied with
this, the enraged sailmaker continued assaulting him more like a wild
beast than a rational being. He foamed at the mouth; his usually
stony eyes glared horribly, dilated, and seemed starting from their

caverns; while his lips were livid as his face, and were drawn tightly
back from the teeth. He jumped on the prostrate man, kicking him
about the head, face, and body with his heavy sea-boots, and exerting
all his immense strength. He knelt on the poor man's chest, and
throttled him with one hand whilst hammering away with the other.

By this time the officers and many of the crew had rushed to the
spot. Certainly they were not a moment too soon for saving the
steward's life; but it was not till Eli Boggs had his arms nearly
broken by repeated blows from an iron belaying-pin wielded by the
third mate, that his deadly grasp became relaxed. When at length
dragged from his helpless victim, he turned like a madman upon those
endeavouring to restrain him, and was not secured in hand and foot
irons before seriously hurting several of them.

In consequence of this affair he was kept a week in confinement;
then disrated and sent before the mast—*i.e.*, reduced to a common
seaman.

Henceforth all hands, fore and aft, were against him, and he was
against all hands. Although there were powerful men—brave and
active—in the forecastle, all seemed to dread the outcast's herculean
strength; no one appeared anxious to get in his way as he strode
moodily about the decks, muttering threats of vengeance against
every one on board. Dark, savage, and mysterious, this disagreeable
character seemed admirably suited for the sanguinary and merciless
pirate it became rumoured that he had been.

One exception there was to the otherwise universal detestation
in which the disrated sailmaker was held by his shipmates. Friday,
the black cook, was that exception.

This coloured individual was not one of those popular sort of
funny, good-tempered, evangelical niggers one may hear of at Exeter

Hall, where, every now and then, at appropriate opportunities, a "stage property" kind of negro, well got up in white choker, &c., is produced, and whose appearance is hailed with a mild and generally benignant enthusiasm, followed by a corresponding flow of contribu-

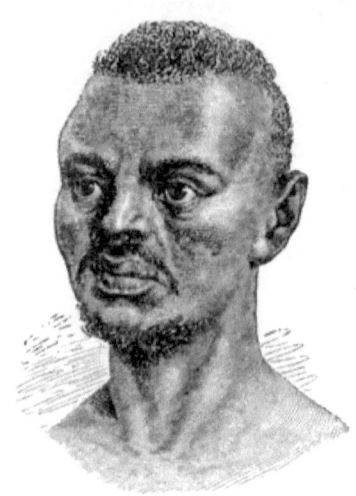

FRIDAY.

tions—well meant, no doubt, but indefinite, very Far from being of this style of show darky, Friday was a very low type of African; and if Robinson Crusoe's man had been anything like him, that celebrated castaway would certainly have preferred seeing him eaten by the cannibals.

The ferocious attack on the steward seemed to delight the cook beyond measure; it may be that some quarrel existed between the two—an occurrence by no means uncommon in the case of individuals holding their respective berths on board ship. Ever afterwards Friday appeared to entertain a profound admiration for Eli

Boggs. The black savage and the savage white, as they became more and more estranged from the rest of the crew, daily increased the friendship that had arisen between them in consequence of their similar sympathies and nature. In the dog-watches, and often during the calm tropical nights, the two might be seen yarning together—at least, Friday was always the listener, and many were his hoarse peals of laughter when particularly amused by his comrade's observations. Several of the crew had overheard the conversation at such times, and they declared that the few words they had caught were of the most bloodthirsty and ferocious import, seemingly relative to former deeds of the narrator.

One night, shortly after the former sailmaker had taken up his quarters in the forecastle, a great uproar was heard by the watch on deck. Before they could ascertain the cause, they were astonished to see the watch below come tumbling up, half dressed, and more or less just as they had turned in after being relieved a couple of hours before. These men had been hard worked during their hours of duty, shortening sail and making all snug aloft for increasing wind and squally weather; therefore, it was quite certain that something very extraordinary must have taken place to rouse them out at three bells, before their watch below had half terminated. Not only were these facts well calculated to excite the surprise of those on deck, but the pale, terrified appearance of the disturbed men plainly told them that something serious was the matter.

Attracted by the clamour, the officer of the watch came running forward, yet, although his language was rather more forcible than elegant, it was some little time before he could elicit the fact that the affrighted watch below had been driven on deck by something which they all declared to be a ghost. The officer's energetic protestations were uselessly employed to pacify the men and induce them to re-enter the forecastle and turn in again; he was, therefore, obliged to send for a lantern, rouse out the boatswain, and institute a search.

When Mr. Pipes arrived on deck, armed with a huge globe lamp, and evidently by no means delighted at being disturbed, he soundly rated each superstitious sailor as he held the light close to his face whilst cursing him. The boatswain was a fine sturdy specimen of a British seaman; but, in spite of the authority he usually possessed over the crew, not a man moved to obey his reiterated order to go below.

"Why, you cowardly lubbers!" said he; "d'ye call yourselves men, eh?"

Then, after consigning their eyes and limbs to certain warm regions, he continued—

"Poor little dears! They should have brought their Ma's to sea to take care of 'em and keep off bogies, *they should.* Stand clear, there! Let me put you to bed again—you great, big, hulking hinfants—like Joe Bowse's hairy hinfants you are, I guess, about six feet bigger than a man. Come along, then! Naughty ghosts to frighten little hinnocents!"

Saying which, he entered the forecastle, followed by a couple of men who had mustered up sufficient courage to accompany him, and whose frightened, shivering appearance contrasted oddly enough with their muscular frames, bronzed features, and great bushy beards.

The first object that caught the eye of the boatswain was the black cook, huddled up in a corner of his bunk, livid—or, rather, leaden-coloured—with fear, and muttering incoherently to himself, while his large goggle eyes seemed bursting from their yellow sockets.

Some moments elapsed ere the unhappy nigger could be brought to his senses; even then he could only ejaculate—

"Fetish! Fetish! Obi man! Dat's him; dat's him!"

Upon looking in the direction indicated, and lifting his lantern as high as possible, the boatswain saw Eli Boggs, to all appearance fast asleep and blissfully oblivious to all the troubles of his watch-mates. Before, however, the searchers could make a movement towards him, they were startled and terribly alarmed by the following sepulchral exclamation—

" Friday, tell no lies ! It was not Eli Boggs, but I, who spoke."

Even the stalwart boatswain now became infected with superstitious fear.   That hollow, ghostly voice came from the darkest end
of the black cook's berth ; but, when the three explorers overhauled
that part, nothing could be seen, though one of the men afterwards
affirmed that he had seen a dark shadow flit swiftly through the forecastle.

The two sailors rushed back on deck, but their leader went up to
Eli Boggs where he lay calmly sleeping in his bunk right forward in
" the eyes " of the ship.   It took several rough shakes to awake him,
and when he comprehended that the boatswain accused him of playing
the ghost to frighten his shipmates, he swore a savage oath, and then
rolled over to sleep again, exclaiming,

" Bo'sun, don't bother me with sich tarnation stiff yarns !   I
kalkerlate it's my next wheel, an' I want to sleep."

Even as these words were dying away, a scornful laugh sounded
from the darker part of the forecastle ; but as the boatswain in alarm
let fall his lantern, he was unable to see who or what it was.   Groping
his way to the forecastle door, he fell over the raised wooden grooves
in which it slid, and scattered the assembled crew by his sudden
appearance, as well as by the noise of his fall.

By this time the ship was in a state of confusion fore and aft.
The captain had been called, and he now gave orders to turn all
hands out and muster them on the quarter-deck.   This was soon
accomplished, for nearly all were there already.

The ship was at this time in the latitude of the Cape of Good
Hope, and as the wind—which had now increased to a moderate gale
—whistled and sang through the cordage, the men who had been
frightened half clad from their berths shivered and shook with the

cold.   Two deck lanterns were lighted and hung up at the break
of the poop, where Captain Grey then proceeded to address
his crew.

"Men," said he, "what is the cause of this disturbance? Has
any one been skylarking with the watch below?"

"No, sir! It's a ghost aboard. A Jonah in the ship," &c. &c.,
came in chorus from the hands.

The officer of the watch, having communicated with the commander, called upon the boatswain to stand forward and tell what he
had seen. When Mr. Pipes had described the incident that took
place in the forecastle, Jack Jigger, the man who had seen the shade
or shadow, was called upon for *his* statement.

"Well, my man, what did you see?" the captain asked.

"Ay, ay, sir; I'll jist be afther tellin' what I seed. 'Sure, thin,
I follered th' bo'sun inter th' fo'ks'le, an', all ov a suddint, jist while
we was a-lookin' at the docthor, ([1]) what should I hear but th' same
ghost as druv us out ov th' fo'ks'le. 'Friday,' it says, 'yer black son
ov a sea cook, don't tell no lies, or I'll carry yer away on th' end ov
me grains.([2])   It was me as spake, it wasn't Eli Boggs, nivir th' bit.'
Well, sir, axin' yer pardin, I makes bould t' say as how any one aboard
would ha' felt his heart go up an' down like a brig's boom in a calm
—jist as mine did; so I slews round, an' gave sheet t' get on deck
again; but, as I tried to, dowse me toplights! if I didn't see the ghost
a-makin' off, with his tail atween his legs, an' his toastin'-fork over
his right shoulder——"

"Why, how's that, my man? I am told that you merely said
you thought you saw a shadow," interrupted the captain.

([1]) The ship's cook.   ([2]) A kind of harpoon used for spearing fish.

"Thrue, sir. But I was kind ov flabergasted thin; now I'll take me Bible oath I seed the ghost as I said afore—horns, tail, an' toastin'-fork. His eyes were more nor a foot wide, an' shinin' like a couple ov red-hot sixty-eight pound shot in the middle ov a cask ov gunpowther. His——"

"Stop a moment, Jack Jigger," said Captain Grey. "If the ghost had its back turned, and you could see its tail, how could its face be visible at the same time?"

After a momentary hesitation, the Irish sailor continued—

"Why, d'ye see, sir, I saw its face first. It turned round an' looked at me as it was runnin' away. Yes, by Saint Pathrick! I'll swear t' that. His tail was about three fathom long, an' th' end ov it was coiled round an' round his neck. All ov a suddent he vanished in th' middle ov a flash of flamin' lightnin', an' th' sthrong smell ov brimstone made me kind ov so as I felt as if I'd been keelhauled, an' was bein' rolled in a water-cask."

At this moment the ghost interrupted the description.

"Ha, ha, ha!" A long and Satanic laugh seemed to come from the weather side of the poop, close to the captain, when not a soul could be seen, though Jack Jigger and several others declared that they had seen a great black shape, with fiery eyes and flaming breath, far away on the weather quarter.

The consternation of the crew was now intense. They thought themselves doomed—they thought of the "Flying Dutchman" and a hundred other sailor ghost stories; and, to add to their troubles, the weather was rapidly getting worse, with strong squalls, heavy sea, and threatening appearances.

Captain Grey turned pale for a moment, and his courageous spirit quailed a little, but he sharply cried—

" Now, my lads, who was it that laughed ? Pass him to the front."

A short silence succeeded. Then that bitter, mocking laugh rang from the maintop, and, barely heard above the howling of the wind, came these words—

" I spoke—Captain Grey. You—are all—doomed !"

Although the master of the *Imogene* now felt awed by the supernatural mystery, he still tried to encourage his men by appearing calm and fearless. He knew perfectly well that all hands were on deck before him, but, in order to prevent the crew reflecting upon the same fact, he shouted in a quick, commanding tone—

" Two hands jump up aloft, one on each side, and find out who that is in the maintop. Some of you run for'ard, men, and see that no one comes down by the stays."

Nearly all hands ran along the main-deck, but not a man moved to go aloft.

" D'ye hear there, men ?" the captain cried again ; but no one replied.

Then, turning to his chief officer, he said—

" Mr. Bowline, a couple of officers must go aloft ; the hands are too frightened. Bear a hand, if you please, for we must take in another reef directly, and we shall never be able to do it while the men are in this state."

" Ay, ay, sir," replied the mate. " There does seem to be something more than the two ta'gallant stun'sails in the top ; but it is impossible to see clearly through the gloom."

Then, very complacently, he requested his subordinates—the second and third mates—to fulfil the captain's order.

These two were scarcely less perturbed than the rest of the crew, for sailors—whether before the mast or on the quarter-deck—

THE GHOST ON BOARD THE "IMOGENE."

are all superstitious, and in this case even the most sceptical would
have been either frightened or nearly convinced that ghosts were not
mythical.   The officers hesitated for a moment between their fears
and duty, but then the third mate—a blue-eyed, curly-haired, handsome young sailor—ran to the lee main-rigging, turning to the second
officer as he did so, and saying—

"Come, Mister Snatchblock, let us show the men the way aloft
—ghost or no ghost.   I'll go up to loo'ard."

The second mate sprang to the weather shrouds.   When the
crew saw their officers going first, two of them felt sufficiently
encouraged to follow.

The maintop was reached ; but no one could be found there ;
though the third mate ran up to the cross-trees to make sure, not
the vestige of a human being could be discovered aloft.   Before
the searchers had descended to the deck, the terrible visitor was
heard, seemingly in the foretop—

"Ha, ha, ha !" it laughed, above the whistling of the gale; "ha,
ha, ha !"

"There it is !   There it is !" cried several of the crew, and, their
courage having been raised by the action of their officers, they began
to ascend the fore-rigging, thinking that they saw a man crouching
in the top, which, however, they had no sooner reached than the
ghost was heard under the long-boat, amidships.

Still that awful laugh was heard, first in one place and then in
another, while the night became so dark that it was impossible to
detect anything aloft.   The affrighted crew were in a great state of
terror, imagining a supernatural being in every tall shadow that
appeared through the haze.

Scarcely a man on board doubted but that an evil spirit had

.taken possession of the ship. The captain went below to consult with his officers : the men were all huddled together forward, listening to their favourite spokesman.   Eli Boggs and Friday were left to themselves; the former seeming the only man on board not frightened at the ghost, whilst the latter kept close by his side as though he were a protecting god, and, dumb with terror, listened to his horrible ghostly tales, related in a voice loud enough for nearly all the crew to hear.   Eli Boggs, at length tired of exciting his shipmates' fears, went below, whither he was quickly followed by his sable friend.   As they disappeared, Jack Kelson, the forecastle oracle, addressed his cowering audience —

"Look'ee here, my hearties," said he, "there's a Jonah aboard this ship!   It's no use backing and filling about it, no how; there's a Jonah aboard; an' I makes bould to say as how you've all been heddified by a-hearing ov his familyar speerit skylarking fore an' aft the old 'hooker's' decks, an' dodging about her spars."

"What's the matter, Bill?" the speaker suddenly asked a man, who belonged to the watch below, and whose teeth chattered as he started up (being only half clad), and replied—

"Ja-Ja-Jack, I sa-saw the ghost!"

"Where? where?" shouted a dozen voices.

"Wa-walking aft under the lee of the ma-main trysail," said Bill.

The ghost, however, had disappeared, and nothing could be seen except when an occasional straggling ray of moonlight would penetrate the flying scud overhead, and raise shadows that changed and played with every roll of the plunging vessel.

Jack Kelson resumed his address—

"Well, messmates, it's no use playing fanny-naddy not no more. It's proved there's a Jonah on the ship's articles, an'———"

" There it is! I'm sure I saw it," interrupted another sailor, pointing up aloft.

All hands looked as directed, and several thought that they could see something, especially Jack Jigger, who once more began to describe the ghost's very unfavourable appearance. The men were thoroughly unnerved, and were startled at every sound or shadow.

At length Jack Kelson continued—

" Look'ee here, my boys; what we want to find out is—who's the Jonah ? When I was afore the mast in the old *Kent*, on a v'yage to Moulmein, we had a Jonah aboard. Well, shiver my timbers! if we didn't find him out, an' knock off work till the skipper put into the hisland of Flores an' sent him ashore. Howsomedever, there was no familyar speerit (as the skollards say) in that case; on'y we got nothing but dead calms, or gales ov wind lashed together an' blowing right on end. Either the canvas was flapping for want ov wind, or else it was blown out ov the bolt-ropes with too much ; an' at last we lost our three topmasts, jib-boom, an' nearly every sail on board. A long-shore beach-comber, who shipped as Jemmy Ducks, (¹) was the Jonah—'cos why ? 'Cos he was always a-sulking and a mutterin' to hisself like Eli Boggs there (pointing in the direction of the fore-castle). I remember I was once quartermaster in an opium smuggler, an' there we pitched a Jonah overboard—a whinin', snivellin' sort ov a lubber, who was always a-makin' long draw-bucket faces, an' speechifyin' like a Methody parson to a school ov niggers in Jimaky. Howsomedever, that's neither here nor there. Now, I means to say that Eli Boggs, or the nigger, or the pair ov 'em,'s the Jonah here ! Consequendly, if we all stick together, an' knock off work unless the

---

(¹) A sobriquet given to the landsman who attends to the poultry on board ship.

skipper puts into the Cape an' lands 'em, I guess we'll make him do it ; an' so we'll part company with the Jonah, ghost an' all. Therefore, I calls upon you to speak up, my hearties. Speak up, an' let us see if we're all goin' to pull in the same boat ! "

Several men had their say, and all agreed to act as Jack Kelson advised, deputing him to state their determination to the captain. However, before this could be done, all hands were called to put the ship about, the wind having veered to the south, rendering it necessary to place her upon the other tack in order to lay her course.

The men were accordingly seen to their stations by the officers ; arrangements were made to take in another reef directly the manœuvre had been completed ; then the chief mate reported from his station on the forecastle to his superior on the poop, "All ready, sir ! "

The captain ordered the helm to be put down, giving the command, " Hard a-lee ! " when the jib and fore-sheets were let go. As the ship flew up in the wind, and her sails began to shake, he gave the order, " Raise tacks and sheets ! "

So far well and good ; but no sooner had the courses commenced to flap, than the men stationed at the main braces received, as they thought, the command from the captain, " Mainsail haul ! " The lee braces were cast loose, and round flew the main-yard ; but, having been hauled too soon, while the wind was yet broad on the weather bow, the ship missed stays and would not come round.

Captain Grey ran aft in a passion, and soundly rated the men for having hauled the main-yard without orders. This they denied, for each of them had plainly heard the words, " Mainsail haul ! "

The after-yards were filled again, and when the ship had gathered good head-way, the attempt to " stay " her was renewed.

" Put the helm down !" the captain sang out.

" Hard down it is, sir !" duly responded the man at the wheel ; but scarcely had he shifted a dozen spokes when he received an order to " Put the helm up again !"

The ship came up and shook in the wind, but, the helm catching her as it was shifted, she fell off again, just as the skipper shouted, " Tacks and sheets !"

The ghost had interfered with the captain's orders as before, and the manœuvre was again foiled ; there was not time to try it any more, for the squalls now came so strong that it was absolutely necessary to reef down without delay. Orders were given to clew up the mainsail, brail in the spanker, and let go the topsail halyards, so as to " wear" ship while the yards were clewed down for reefing.

Although the ghost still interfered, and many of the crew swore that they had seen it—each man giving a different account—it was not able to prevent the success of the fresh manœuvre, as the captain, after seeing the helm put up, stood by the main braces himself, and kept the after-yards shaking, whilst the chief officer trimmed the fore-yards as the ship fell oft before the wind and came-to on the other tack.

The crew were now ordered aloft to take in another reef. Not a man moved to obey. Then Jack Kelson went to the captain and told him that all hands refused duty unless he put the ship before the wind and ran for the Cape of Good Hope, in order to land Eli Boggs and the black cook.

In any other instance Captain Grey would have taken prompt measures to suppress the slightest symptoms of mutiny ; but the present case was too exceptional and extraordinary. It was so palpable that the ship could not be navigated under the circum-.

stances—officers and men alike being infected with the gravest superstition, and incapacitated with dread of the ghost—that he felt justified
in yielding to the unanimous wish of the crew. After a few moments'
consultation with his officers, he gave orders to square away the
yards, shake out the reefs that had been previously taken in, and
run before the wind on a direct course to the Cape.

During two days the *Imogene* scudded before the gale, and
then the great square top of Table Mountain loomed up above the
clouds, obscuring the horizon ahead.

Meanwhile, the ghost had continued its malignant pranks, till
every one on board was at his wit's end, though nothing had
transpired to elucidate the mystery.   Watch and watch became a
farce, for all hands kept the deck during the interval until the land
was made, Eli Boggs and Friday being the only exceptions ; the
former, seemingly delighted at the supernatural visitation, was often
seen chuckling to himself when his shipmates were terrified more
than usual.   He regularly turned in during his watch below, having
the forecastle entirely to himself and Friday, who, since the first
alarm, had followed, cowed and timorous, at his heel.   The unfortunate African seemed totally bereft of what little reason he ever
possessed, and, being quite unfit for duty, one of the seamen took his
place in charge of the galley and coppers.

At last Table Bay opened out to the view of the weary crew,
and made their hearts beat with exultation at the prospect of getting
rid of the ghost or Jonah.   Before, however, the ship could enter the
bay, it was necessary to place her on a wind and beat up to the distant
anchorage ; to do so it was requisite that the topsails should be reefed
again, and the weather became so bad that it was impossible to reach
the harbour during five days.

The main-topsail had been reefed, and the hands, with the exception of two still busy at the weather earing, were laying out to reef the mainsail, when the ghost came to disturb them again. One of those still on the topsail yardarm happened to be the third mate ; he was just getting inside the lift, and feeling for the foot-rope, when the unearthly cry resounded in his ear—

"Die! Die! Your life is mine!"

Uttered, as these words seemed to be, by some invisible spirit, they were quite sufficient to unnerve the bravest of the *Imogene's* crew. Startled while in so precarious a position, the young officer lost his hold and fell from the yard. Singularly enough, Eli Boggs, being on the lee quarter of the main-yard, was knocked off by the third mate, who struck against him in his fall. Both were picked up on deck, mortally injured.

The third mate expired early on the morning of the day succeeding the accident. Captain Grey and the second mate (the dying youth's particular friend) were ministering at his bedside till the end, more like tender women than such great rough seamen. The last words of the dying officer were, " My mother! oh, my mother !"

Long may that desolate, fair-haired, gentle mother wait for the return of her darling sailor son—curly and fair-haired too ; and vainly may she watch in the gloaming from her peaceful cottage door ; but never—never till the sea gives up its dead—may they meet again ; for the boy she loved far better than worldly joy, or life itself, lies among the tangled weeds, and strange, slimy, unknown monsters, fathoms—hundreds of fathoms deep—on the treacherous ocean's bed. Never more may her fingers play lovingly with those almost girlish tresses, for slowly, monotonously, and lifelessly are they washed backwards and forwards, to and fro, by the heaving of the sea upon his resting-place.   That brave, merry, generous life has fled for ever, and what remains of its earthly tabernacle is still and quiet—so quiet—at the bottom of the sea.   Curious, gigantic marine plants twist and twine—loathsome creatures creep and crawl—about all that is left of the hapless victim to a malignant though punished revenge!

The day after the unfortunate young officer's body had been consigned to the deep, the weather moderated, and the ship was enabled to anchor before Cape Town.   Eli Boggs was carried ashore to the hospital, whither his friend Friday attended him.   Three fresh hands were engaged, and the *Imogene* proceeded on her voyage, no longer haunted, the ghost having entirely disappeared; whereat Jack Kelson took great credit unto himself.

The death of Eli Boggs took place a few days later.   He became conscious shortly before dissolution, and able, for the first time since the accident, to say a few words to his only friend and sympathiser.

"Oh, Massa — Obi Massa!   Guess you's a-gwine to die!" howled the subdued Friday, as he saw the shadow of death stealing athwart the features of his sinister associate.

"Wall, I kal-ker-late I'm a—a gone coon," Eli Boggs cried with an expiring effort.   "Revenge—re-venge, Friday.   I—I scotched—my own back—I—reckon.   Sorry now.   Friday—you —can—tell 'em—I'm a—a——," and as Friday bent his ear to the dying man's mouth, he just caught the word " ventriloquist."

THE LOG.

January 10th.

11*h.* 30*m. p.m.*—As I finished the ghost story, there was a simultaneous burst of merriment—in which even old Jack Backstay joined —at the absurd and ludicrous appearance of surprised mortification and disappointment spreading over the doctor's countenance. But a moment before he had been all smiles and grins; was chuckling to, and evidently very well satisfied with, himself. But to look on this picture and then on that! it was too absurd, and we literally roared with laughter. It was the break applied to an over-sanguine temperament. Old Jack took the matter much more philosophically, and his bristly moustache was merely elevated a little in pity and contempt for those who did not believe in Davy Jones and the Flying Dutchman

After all, the doctor had some very strong arguments on his side. No sooner had he somewhat recovered from the mortification into which my unexpected *dénouement* had thrown him, than he said—

" It is all very well to laugh, my boys, but if you do not believe in ghosts or spirits, pray tell me what becomes of the souls of the dead, and where they go to during the interval between death and the resurrection ? None of you are Roman Catholics, and so, of course, you don't believe in purgatory ; and I should very much like to know how you account for the spirits of the departed. They cannot go to heaven, because the last day—the day of resurrection—

THE CREEK I DISCOVERED.

is to place them either there or somewhere else. They cannot go to
that particular somewhere else, for the same reason. Again, it seems
to be absolutely necessary that the resurrection of the body should
take place before the soul can be condemned or rewarded. Therefore, if the spirits of the dead are neither in heaven, hell, nor purgatory, I say that they are still on earth, and defy any one to
disprove either that opinion or the theory of a spirit-world among us,
especially as demons, devils, and spirits are so frequently mentioned
in the Bible."

But there is no occasion to turn this book into a theological,
metaphysical, and psychological treatise; although upon the night in
question our conversation lasted long and animated, and partook of

that rather dry and abstruse triune nature. I think the doctor came off victorious, after all, for none of us could answer his triumphant query as to the whereabouts and disposal, or qualities, of departed spirits during the interregnum.

Of course that night the doctor did his best to convince his berth-mate (old Jack Backstay) as to the veritable existence of ghosts. I have not the slightest doubt that he had a capital subject to work upon, but whether he succeeded or failed in impressing his own peculiar opinions, I cannot exactly state, although, from my berth next to theirs, I heard Mr. Backstay's frequent "Ay, ay!" (the only variety of response he ever used being in the difference of tone) to a very late hour, and believe that it continued mechanically, long after he had himself gone to sleep, and the monotonous sound had sent me to the arms of Morpheus likewise.

January 11*th.*

This day being warm and fine, we took a long excursion ashore, and along the wild sea-beach. Moreover, we went in a more comfortable style than previously, for, having found out that the water was deep all around the wretched mud-bank upon which we were fixed, we had hired a comfortable Chinese boat, with a spacious thatched covering amidships. Whilst out to-day, I came most unexpectedly upon a very romantic little creek, literally thronged with vast flocks of the large rice-bird and every description of wild water-fowl.

This was an opportunity not to be neglected. Rejoining my friends, I took them to the spot, and we thereupon incontinently did decide to have an afternoon's sport—to us, but death to them— among the feathery host rushing wildly screaming in alarm above our heads.   Returning, therefore, to the *Fortuna* for our guns, we divided our party of five between her gig and the Chinese *sanpan*, and then proceeded to the scene of action.   What sport we did have!   From fifty to sixty brace of rice-birds, and over twenty brace of various kinds of duck, were bagged that afternoon ; and the victims, be it remembered, were not fatted denizens of an English preserve—too lazy to fly away, and too tame to keep clear of the muzzles of the guns—but, upon the contrary, were really wild, wary, and suspicious game, though incredibly plentiful.   The guns kept banging away, and the birds coming splash all around us, until we became quite tired of it.   The rice-bird—of a pure white colour, and closely similar in appearance to a young crane—is a most delicious food, and all hands on board the *Fortuna* feasted upon it till the end of that cruise.

It was quite dark by the time we gave up shooting and thought of returning on board, and then it was easier said than done, for a singular circumstance had taken place.   The day had been very hot —unusually so for the time of year—and when we ordered the boatmen to pull for the schooner, upon looking round for her, and looking in vain, we, for the first time, became aware that the heat had produced a most extraordinary crepusculous state of the atmosphere —air, land, and water being utterly confused, blended together, and subjected to a peculiar sort of metamorphosis similar to that produced during the mirage.   Beneath the mat awning of the boat in which I was the heat was so close and stifling that we took it by turns in lying down outside upon the top of the cover, which was not strong enough to bear more than one at a time.   Here, one after the other, I, Esmond, and Mr. Lawrence smoked our cheroots and took it easy whilst the boat's crew pulled about in search of the schooner, which they did

SHOOTING RICE-BIRDS.

not succeed in finding for at least a couple of hours. It was awfully jolly, that return to the stanch old *Fortuna*. It was just the sort of warm, sultry, dreamy tropical night to give oneself up to utter laziness, and certainly, upon the top of the boat's little house, we had our *otium*, but *sine* the *dignitate*.

Our worthy long-tailed tars, becoming sensibly affected by the weird, ghastly, supernatural sort of aspect of the evening, began to feel superstitious—a failing to which they, in common with their compatriots generally, were by no means strangers. Therefore, in order, I suppose, to encourage themselves, and drive the gloomy fancies from their Celestial minds, they started one of those wailing, melancholy, long-drawn dirges, in which the heart of the Chinese man doth largely rejoice. This style of singing is entirely imaginative, extemporary, and *à l'improviste*, and the quavering, long-drawn, sad-toned falsetto notes in which it is sung are very peculiar, and have a delightfully lulling, soothing effect, when their sorrowful melody sounds echoing over the still dark waters of the silent night. The dirge consisted of one verse, continuously repeated, in somewhat like the following form:—

> " Oh, spirits, spirits, spirits of the vasty deep,
> Watch o'er us, guard us, from all danger keep !
> From demons, devils, wicked beings of the air,
> Save us, ye gods ! and hear our evening prayer !"

We should have been still longer in getting on board, had we not suddenly heard the well-known tones of Jack Backstay's voice come rolling, echoing, and reverberating over the misty waters to us, followed by the scarcely louder roar of one of the *Fortuna's* swivel guns. Mr. Backstay and the doctor, in the ship's boat, having arrived first, considerately began to signal for us.

By the time that the dinner things were cleared away, it was very near eight bells, so we got into our places, leaving *the* chair to our friend the doctor, whose turn at story-telling came this night.

8*h. p.m.*--As the echo of the bell died lazily away in the murky atmosphere above, the doctor just cleared his throat with a few sips of Esmond's " particular ; " then, whilst we lighted our manillas, stirred up the fire, and stretched ourselves out at ease, he began to spin his yarn.

"STUCK UP."

AN ADVENTURE WITH AUSTRALIAN BUSHRANGERS.

CERTAINLY the title of this story is not one of the most refined that could be found. It is very decidedly more forcible than elegant; but then, it is the exact name for that which took place, and which I am going to narrate. It is not English, it is a colonialism; and out in Australia, where people get coarse by "roughing it," such harsh and pithy expressions become common.

I had been several years in New South Wales—mind, I paid my own passage out there—but had not yet made my fortune; in fact, had become reduced to my last piece of gold, and was just beginning to regret having left ould Ireland and emigrated, when I found myself, one beautiful summer's evening, at the sheep station at Gundigi, on the high road to Naomi Creek from West Maitland. I had left the latter place some days previous, to join in the rush for the creek of the plentiful name, where gold had just been discovered —it was rumoured, in large quantity.

Gundigi was a wretched little place on Cooper's Creek, but the sight of it was welcome—very; for I was hungry, and, besides, tired of solitary companionship with myself. The station contained three buildings—the dwelling of the sheep proprietor and his servants, which consisted of a large, rambling, irregular-shaped log and bark

I 2

hut; besides a blacksmith's shanty, and a rough bark cottage—the Gundigi public-house and hotel.

Of one thing—a kind and hearty welcome—the weary wanderer in the *bush* is sure, whenever he is lucky enough to tumble across the shanty of a squatter in the wilderness. Consequently, I was received with hospitality; and so, instead of continuing on my way to Naomi Creek, determined to pass the night at the station. I had become tired of passing the nights either alone in my blanket upon the bare ground, or, what was almost, if not quite as bad, at some wretched hovel of the aborigines. Only the night before it had been my lot to pass it with a couple of *black fellows*, whose utterly miserable condition I shall never forget. Poor wretches! So far as my experience goes, they are certainly the most degraded type of humanity.

Just as the fiery red sun was setting in the blood-red crimson of an Australian sunset, all hands assembled in the big room of the Gundigi hotel. The company consisted of fourteen white men in all, besides a nigger cook of African race, and an Australian *black fellow*, who acted as attendant. Besides the proprietor of the sheep station—a Mr. Williams—there was "Myall Tom," the landlord; Remi Shmidt, a German-Jew pedlar, well known in the *bush*; two "new chums," just arrived from England, with plenty of money, and out prospecting for a likely spot to settle upon; and myself; the rest of the party being the drovers, shepherds, &c., of Mr. Williams.

This gentleman was a *savant* of reputation, and whilst out in the bush some months previous, following his scientific pursuits in company with Dr. Beattie, of Melbourne, went through a most extraordinary adventure. I had heard something of this, and now, whilst waiting for dinner, having got into conversation with Mr. Williams, I received from him the following account of it.

WHERE THE DOCTOR PASSED THE PREVIOUS NIGHT.

It appears that they had gone far into the *bush*, and away from the settlements, upon a scientific and surveying expedition, quite alone. All went well with them until one evening, when they had penetrated to a very singularly formed gully, where they made up their minds to pass the night. Thoughtless of danger, they had just made arrangements for cooking their supper, when, from the top of the cliffs above and around them, whiz came a shower of spears, and at the same instant, the loud, hideous yells which burst upon their startled ears, told them that a tribe of aborigines were besetting them. By a providential movement they had unwittingly saved their lives, for the *black fellow* never misses his aim with the spear—in the use of which he is wonderfully expert—but it seems that at the very moment when the deadly weapons were launched against them by the unseen foe, they had both thrown themselves flat upon the ground, tired out with the day's toil, and to rest themselves while waiting for the kettle to boil. Very fortunately, again, a lucky inspiration preserved their lives. Mr. Williams had once seen the intense delight with which a party of natives had beheld the saltatory exercise of some Europeans, and, springing to his feet, he instantly began to dance and hop away, not as *if* his life depended upon it, but because it *did;* at the same time calling to his companion—

" Doctor! doctor! for God's 'sake dance! It may save our lives ! "

" Dance! but I can't! I don't know how," cried the unfortunate doctor, wringing his hands, and gazing piteously around.

But at that moment whiz came another spear, only missing his vitals by the spring he had made after his companion.

" Try," said the latter, and further pressing was not required, for the doctor saw that no spears came at his dancing friend, and forthwith he began to hop and jump about, in a way that caused the savages above to scream and whoop with delight.

For more than one whole hour those two unfortunate men went on with their exertions. It was, indeed, a dance for life! From the gully there was no escape but by the way they had entered it, and their enemies were close above.

It was a frightful sight! Those black, hideous faces, with their savage eyes glaring down upon them from the tangled vegetation above—the glaring eyes, the hideous forms, and the brandished weapons made more formidable by the redly gleaming flashes of the firelight. The horrid yell of the Australian echoed long and loudly through the caves and winding passage of the gully; but though the alarming sound made their hearts quiver, it proved, in the end, another providential circumstance, by which their lives were saved : for it is uncertain whether the savages would have killed or taken them prisoners when they had become too exhausted to continue that grotesquely horrible performance. Those vociferous yells, however, chanced to reach the ears of a gold escort passing on their way from the newly-discovered gold-fields at Lonely Gully. Attracted by the loud hubbub, they turned aside and hastened to the spot. Absorbed with their victims, the natives were unaware of the escort's approach, and the first thing that they knew of it was the last with many of their number. *Crack ! crack !* went the rifles and the rapid detonations of the Colt's revolvers. A dozen *black fellows* were killed, the rest fled howling into the dense scrub, where the mounted constabulary could not follow, and the two *savants* were carried off in safety, more dead than alive.

A repast of tea, *damper*, roast beef and corned beef, Hollands gin and Australian peaches, had just been spread upon the table, and

A DANCE FOR LIFE.

to my keen appetite seemed of almost Sybarite luxury, when, lo! the first dig of each knife was abruptly arrested, and each uplifted morsel fell untasted to the plate.

The door had been suddenly thrown open, and two—*only two*—wild-looking, bearded fellows sprang into the room.

It was not so much the fact of their unceremonious entrance that troubled us (if the intruders had liked springing, we would have let them spring with all our hearts), but, confound them! each held a brace of deadly large-sized Colt's revolvers at our heads!

The moment they appeared, "Myall Tom" made a move as though he would put his hand beneath the counter of the bar, only a foot or two behind his chair, as he sat at the head of the table. I knew that a loaded revolver was lying there on a little shelf, for I had been admiring its workmanship only a short time before dinner. The tallest of our two unwelcome guests, however, observed the action at once, and his brilliant eyes glittered with a fierce, lurid light, as one of his raised six-shooters gave "Myall Tom" the opportunity of gazing down its bore, whilst he shouted, in stern, unfaltering accents—

"Sit still, there, for your life! Move but another inch, and you are a dead man!"

Mine host obeyed, unwillingly, it must be confessed; for his shaggy black brows became closely knitted together, whilst his bull-dog-like countenance quickly assumed a dusky, angry tinge of red. He was a bit of a fighting-man, and not much accustomed to coercion.

As for the rest of our party, all were too surprised for any attempt at either individual or concerted action. Every man sat waiting for some one else to do something; while all attentively eyed the steadily-levelled revolvers. Yes, sure enough the hollow tubes were covering us; we knew that firm fingers were on the triggers, too, and that any attempt at resistance would be certain death to those who first resorted to it; and it was impossible to arrange for a general rush upon our two daring assailants.

Immediately after quieting "Myall Tom," the tallest of the two bushrangers—a man of decidedly elegant and commanding presence —advanced into the centre of the room, closely followed by his companion, and said—

" Now then, gentlemen, I do not wish to put you to any inconvenience, but I have a particular desire for any spare cash or jewellery that you may have about you. I am ' Captain Melville;' my friend is known as ' Dutch Sam.' "

A murmur ran round our subdued circle. The two most famous bushrangers in the whole colony had just been named.

Captain Melville looked the hero of romance, in the pirate-captain or brigand-chief line, to an iota. He was a tall, handsome man, in the prime of life, with dark flashing eyes, long black curls, regular features, and Apollo-like build. His companion was of shorter, but more massive and Herculean frame; and, as far as appearances went, might well have been taken for an even more formidable antagonist than his chief, in spite of the many authentic accounts of the latter's strength and courage.

" Attention, if you please, gentlemen! " continued the noble bushranger. " Step from the table one by one and range yourselves against the wall there. You, Mister ' Myall Tom ' (for I know you), get up first, and come over here, nearest to me. Then the rest form up, side by side, between you and the other corner of the room. Now, then—come along, sir! "

Up went our landlord, sullenly enough, and casting lingering

ENTRANCE OF THE BUSHRANGERS.

glances to where he left his pet revolver. This again attracted
Captain Melville's attention, who sent his companion to look behind
the bar; when the weapon was discovered and duly stuck into the
discoverer's belt, by the side of a formidable " Arkansas toothpick "—
Anglice, a twelve-inch bowie-knife.

There, one by one, shamefully enough, but quite helplessly, we all
took up our respective stations along the wall; till at length there we
stood, the whole fourteen of us, " stuck up " by only *two* men !

As for myself, I can freely say that it went strong against the
grain being thus brought to bay, bullied, and robbed ; but then I had
nothing to lose—only one half-sovereign in the world ; so, each time I
felt it, I managed to suppress the inclination to pull forth my solitary
single-barrelled pistol ; then reason would flatter my wounded pride by
whispering what folly it would be to sacrifice my precious life for ten
shillings ! Glancing at my brothers in misfortune, I saw that night, by
the glaring, flickering light of the half dozen fat lamps, many a bronzed
and manly cheek turn pale and red by turns with rage and shame.
However, at the period of this adventure, bushrangers had become so
much an institution in Australia that a sort of tacit understanding
seemed to exist between them and their victims, as to the quiet submission of the latter when cleverly or daringly taken by *surprise*, in
which case their lives were always spared, whereas resistance would
surely forfeit them. Of course, any open attack by bushrangers was
met bravely enough by the colonists ; but, as the former fought
with halters round their necks, with them generally rested the
advantage.

" Gentlemen," said our polite plunderer, when we had all toed a
line, " here is my handkerchief."

The cambric was produced and held before our eyes for a moment.

Then the captain pushed back all the plates and dishes from one end of the table, and carefully spread it out on the bare board.

"Attention, gentlemen!" said he. "I want you all to deposit whatever you have, in the way of valuables, in this, my handkerchief. Halt, there!" he suddenly roared, bringing his revolver upon a level with his eyes, as half-a-dozen of our number made a move towards him—"halt, there! One at a time, *if you please*, commencing from that end; then, as you deposit, pass over to the other side of the room, and form line again along that wall. Wait a moment, if you will be so kind—wait a moment; don't be too impatient! I just wish to inform you all, before you begin to unburthen yourselves, that after having passed my handkerchief you will *then* be searched, and any man found with hidden property about him will be obliged to step outside and take a walk with me, of fifty yards or so, into the *scrub.*"

A silent pause succeeded this ominous intimation. Then we heard the groaning of Remi the Jew—his cunning, no doubt, had taken alarm, so that he feared trusting to his powers of concealment. After having given us time to ponder his words, Captain Melville continued—

"Now then, gentlemen, step up, if you please!"

What could we do? With the exception of myself and the two "new chums," our party was unarmed. As for the latter, their heavy armament of rifles, Tranter and Adams' revolvers, &c., had, only a short time previous, proved an inexhaustible source of merriment to the rest of us. It need hardly be said that these latest importations from Cockaigne, in the present emergency, failed most ignominiously both in using and preserving their formidable arsenals. Their glittering weapons had attracted the attention of our captors, and, before the captain's last order could be obeyed, he suddenly cried—

"Halt! Wait a moment, gentlemen." ·

Then, turning to his comrade, he continued—

"Here, Sam; just relieve those two 'new chums' of their armament; it might hurt them, they're shaking so."

Standing in a jaunty, elegant attitude at the end of our row, his lip curling with contempt at the timidity of the greenhorns his penetration had so quickly detected, the captain took care of us whilst his partner collected the arms, including two beautiful Westley-Richards' rifles standing in a corner.

Taking up one of these weapons, the audacious fellow admiringly scrutinised it, then took off his slouched hat, made a polite bow to one of the late owners, and said—

"Thank you, Mister 'new chum;' thank you! This is just the very sort of thing we require. We have been wanting new rifles for some time, I and Sam, and these are really beauties."

Then he went to business again, and said—

"Now then, gentlemen, you can step up and take a look at my cambric."

One by one we went through the ordeal, until it came to my turn.

I think that the noble captain must have had his handkerchief made for the express purpose to which he now applied it; for so capacious and ample were its dimensions, that it far more nearly approached a young table-cloth than the civilised article.

As yet, the daring bushrangers had not reaped a goodly harvest for their plucky venture. I do not think there were more than ten or twelve pounds deposited, and this was mostly from Mr. Williams, who, however, had also left a fair-looking diamond ring on the heap.

As I pulled forth my last coin, and threw it down, grimly observing, "There goes the last shot in the locker!" Captain

J

Melville seemed to notice the salt-water twang of the expression, and at the same time his glance rested upon the anchor graven into the back of my right hand, which I had allowed a sailor to execute during the passage out.

"Oh, you're a 'shell-back,' are you? Pick it up again—pick it up again! I've been a sailor myself," said he.

I did not take the trouble to rectify his mistake, neither was I too proud to take back the coin; in fact, I don't mind admitting that the idea of choosing a sovereign instead of the half *did* occur to me; but somehow I did not act upon the inspiration; yet I cannot help thinking that, logically, I had as much right to the sovereign as the bushrangers had; and that, morally, it would have been far better bestowed upon me than upon them. However, at the moment, I was not sufficiently prompt in acting upon such like reflections; pointed revolvers—when they're loaded, and held by desperadoes—having somehow a tendency to correct smart actions.

I passed on, and was followed by the two "new chums." From them the robbers made a goodly haul. The captain's metallic voice, in smooth, gliding, and impressive accents, reminded them of his intimation regarding a promenade into the *scrub*. Then, without further hesitation, the poor Cockneys unbuttoned some of their strange garments (wonderful habiliments these—*à l'Australasian*, according to the London tailors who made them to sell), and forth from hidden parts came most elaborate leathern money-belts. How the marauders did roar with laughter when they saw them! found, too, how well and heavily they were lined.

"Oh! Bill," groaned one to the other, as they ranged their lightened figures by my side, "whyever did you indoose me to leave——"

"Who did? Who did?" interrupted Bill, in hissing and subdued tones. "Who are yer a-talkin' to—eh?"

Bill was evidently the superior spirit of the two.

"Oh, dear! oh, dear!" the other went on. "There goes my father's watch; and the locket—my Marier's locket—the locket of her hown portrait, which she tied round my neck with a blue ribbon——'

"Shut up!" snarled the superior Bill. "Do yer suppose nobody else haint lost nothink? What about the quids I sold the orse and shay for—eh? There they are! What about the hard shiners paid down on the nail for goodwill, lease, fixturs, an' *et ceteras*, for the 'Goose an' Quail'—eh? Pho-oo! Dry up, do!"

And the indignant William relapsed into gloomy silence, having effectually repressed his chum.

Poor snobs! they were little fitted, either by nature or training, for a wild, rough, and roving life. Directly after this adventure they made back-tracks for somewhere near Whitechapel.

When it came to the turn of Remi Shmidt, the Jew, Captain Melville, detecting his palpable descent, said—

"Well, Schnaderach, have you any money?"

"S'help-me-Gott no!" cried he of Hebrew race, in a breath.

"That will do, then. Pass on. We'll have to search you directly—right to the bare buff, remember—and *perhaps* you may not have to take a walk into the *bush* with me," sententiously observed the captain.

"Ach! Gott in himmel! Shtay! shtay! I have a litteel monish in mein pocket, what before I did forgot."

And he fumbled about with his dirty, dingy old clothing.

"Here, Sam; search him," cried the chief, knowing, perhaps, that even the fear of death could not make such an Israelite part with his valuables willingly.

Sam took him into a corner, and, whilst the rest of our party passed before his leader, thoroughly overhauled him.

These were the sounds that issued from that corner :—

"Now, then, my beauty, off with yer coat! It's very rarely you hev sich a walet as me—sich a gentleman walet, I mean—to attend upon yer."

Then we could hear the ripping and tearing, as Sam took his ugly knife and cut out the lining and pockets of the coat.

"Now for your vest. Off with it, yer cent. per cent. darling !"

"Ach! mein Gott! Ach! ach!" groaned the Jew, as a fat pocket-book was taken from an inside pocket of his waistcoat, and the disrobing revealed a digger's belt, which soon followed, and was heavy with gold.

"Boots and stockings !" roared the merciless inquisitor.

Off they came, and out of the venerable hose fell many bank-notes, carefully stitched in linen and placed there for security.

"Oh, holy Moshes! Ach! mein Gott! mein Gott!" whined Remi. "All mein monish! All mein properties—all! Vat skall I do? Oh, Fadder Abrahams !"

So he went on, till, suddenly becoming, I suppose, infuriated at his loss, he sprang upon "Dutch Sam," just as the latter was carrying off the treasures to deposit them in the handkerchief. But the brawny bushranger felled him flat to the floor with one blow of his fist, and the next instant had his revolvers ready in hand in case any of us felt inclined to imitate the Jew.

Picking out the bank-notes, as the miserable Israelite crawled writhing, bleeding, and whining towards him, Captain Melville (who was known to bear some particular animosity against that evilly-reputed race) slowly held them, one by one, in the flame of a lamp, and, as they were consumed, kept up a running commentary of this nature :—

"There goes a fifty, dog of a Jew! This is a twenty, now! Here comes another! What! another fifty? Dear, dear! Schnaderach, how you must have been cheating the poor squatters and diggers," &c.

"Ach, ach! Is id you vat say dat? Ach! you pese von pad mans! Oh, holy Moshes, my monish! You vonts do make von peggars ov me, und I pese sorry I ever see yous. Ach, mein Gott! Der tyvel! py tam! Der shudge skall hang you und der noder mans goots mit der ropes—py tams, he skall! Oh! oh! mein nodes, mein monish! I vill in der babers pud der nodise vat vill cotch you und der oder mans. Oh, I vill vix you mans goot, py Gott! Hoo-oo-oo!" and the Jew fairly broke down, groaning and blubbering, as the last of his notes perished in the flame.

Then the captain addressed "Myall Tom."

"Now, Mister Landlord, *nobblers* all round, if you please; for I cannot leave you, gentlemen, until we have had a glass together to the health and success of our noble selves."

The fellow's cool audacity and touching *bonhomie* affected the rough drovers and shepherds, who gave an applauding shout. Remi went on groaning and muttering strange jargon; I remained indifferent; Mr. Williams and the two "new chums" were alike in gloom, silence, and reserve.

Speaking to the three latter, the bushranger said—

"Gentlemen, do not make yourselves miserable about trifles. You have only lost a few hundreds between you, and have all this continent in which to make more. You have a variety of paths to choose for making your fortune, whilst I am a proscribed and out-lawed man, and have no other way of getting a living. It is my turn to-day, it may be yours to-morrow."

What a philosophical rascal it was!

Turning to the wretched Hebrew, with one jerk of his muscular arm he stood him on his feet; then said—

"Come, Mister Schnaderach, you are well known about these parts, and the landlord will trust you. Order drinks all round!"

"S'help me Gott, nevare-re," began Remi; but his mind soon changed, for the captain had slily drawn his "bowie," and was pricking up his victim with it.

"Ach! Gott in himmel! Shtop! shtop! dat isht mein vlesh vat der nive go indo! I vill order—I vill 'shout' vor der mans!"

"You hear that, landlord!" cried the captain. "Bring the grog along!"

"Well, cap., what'ull yer hev? What's yer liquor?" asked "Myall Tom."

"*Spiders* (a favoured colonial decoction) all round, my hearty."

Spiders were served, and were duly appreciated by all save the "shouter" and the two "new chums:" the Jew could not be pre-vailed upon to imbibe; the two latter made wry faces—when the captain was not looking—as though the drink were vinegar.

"Now then, Sam," said the bushranger to his comrade, when the glasses had passed, "let us be off!"

Then the two backed to the door, Captain Melville favouring us with this parting advice—

"Good-bye, gentlemen! Do not attempt to pursue us; and do not send information of our visit to any neighbouring station for at least a clear twelve hours; should you be imprudent enough to do so,

COOPER'S CREEK.

it will be worse for some of us," and he tapped the butt of his newly
acquired rifle significantly. "Au revoir!"

The threat to search us after depositing in his handkerchief was
only a *ruse* to save time and avoid the danger of searching so many
men; at least, we thought so afterwards.

The noise of their horses' hoofs was the last I heard of the two
famous bushrangers. This story will be remembered by many "old
chums."

After this adventure, instead of going on to Namoi Creek, I
went with the unfortunate Burke's party—who passed Gundigi on the
following day, and nearly all of whom perished in the desert interior—
as far as the head of Cooper's Creek, where gold was fancied to exist.
As far as there I travelled luxuriously on the back of one of the
expedition's camels; then, together with three other gold-seekers, we
branched off, and were pretty successful in finding the precious metal
at a certain spot (shown by the accompanying sketch) on Cooper's
Creek.

THE LOG.

11 p.m.

ELEVEN o'clock was struck by the watchful quartermaster on deck, just as the doctor was upon the point of concluding his story, for he had spun it out with many little explanations and details not necessary for insertion here; so we set to work upon some of the Angel's exquisitely-prepared wild-fowl and pastry, and then to bed, perhaps to dream of bushrangers, *black fellows* with spears and boomerangs, or weighty nuggets of gold, something more considerable than the little beauty, obtained at Cooper's Creek, hanging to the doctor's watch-chain.

January 12th.

During the whole of this day our long-tailed mariners were sorely troubled in spirit, and sourly affected in visage, for Esmond had bitterly offended them by setting them to work. Hitherto, since our sticking on the mud-bank—an operation which I feel morally convinced in my own mind had been purposely executed by our cunning *lowder*—they had had no other work to do than keeping the schooner clean, and had displayed a splendid aptitude for gambling, opium-smoking, and sleeping; not to mention the fact that sundry suspicious-looking *samshoo* jars had been smuggled on board by some of the wild-looking fishermen prowling about, and *samshoo* is an ardent spirit, cunningly extracted from rice, that would kill any ordinary European at fifty paces.

The cause of this day's work consisted in the rising of the tide.

consequent upon a prevalence of easterly winds, of which the skipper took advantage by sending out an anchor astern and trying to heave his vessel off the mud. The attempt proved fruitless ; for our Chinese tars seemed religiously determined not to heave too hard, and I could not help fancying that there was a very suspicious sort of twinkling in their little oblique black eyes as they joyfully resigned themselves once more to cards, *samshoo*, opium, and sleep.

Whilst Esmond was busy on board, the rest of our party took a ramble ashore in a new direction, straight inland.

After several times losing ourselves in the thickets and jungles covering the land about a mile distant from the rugged and marshy coast-line, we at length came upon a charming little bush path, of which I made the sketch shown on the next page, and which we had the curiosity to follow up in order to see where it led.

However, before proceeding upon our voyage of discovery, we halted at the above spot for tiffin ; and only after fortifying ourselves with a tin or two of sardines, some crisp American crackers, and a few bottles of Bass's best, went forward.

We found that the path wound for nearly two miles through a most luxuriant growth of semi-tropical vegetation, which, together with the beautiful wild flowers scattered everywhere around in bounteous profusion, and the rich white clusters of the powerfully-scented and aromatic tree-Magnolia, were very pleasing objects to our senses.

At last we emerged from the fringing belt of woodland, and came upon the open, profusely cultivated country. Far as the eye could reach extended field after field of rice, paddy, esculent roots, and vegetables. Only a few hundred yards before us a singular looking object fixed our attention. It seemed to be a thing about ten feet long and three or four high; living it certainly was, for we could see that it moved, though very slowly. But then the nature of its movements utterly puzzled us; every now and then a portion of its length, at different places, would be elevated above the

rest, and this was somewhat like the undulating motion of a huge serpent; but then, instead of advancing lengthways or end on, it was evidently moving bodily forward, though very slowly, breadth on, its numerous legs giving it a most extraordinary appearance, as it moved in a confused and disconnected manner; whilst for head, or upper part, it presented nothing but an aspect of huge circular patches joined together anyhow. We advanced upon this strange monster, and it gradually began to change its formidable-looking

THE BUSH PATH.

aspect into the harmless appearance shown on the opposite page.

They were rice-planters, wearing great round bamboo hats to protect them from the sun or rain, bare-legged and bare-armed, and up to their knees in the water, covering the exuberantly irrigated fields.

We *chin-chined* with these people, and became great friends. I like those simple, dignified, polite, and well-behaved Chinese peasantry, always providing you can get them alone and away from any of the usurping Tartar dynasty's myrmidons of either the civil

THE RICE-PLANTERS.

(mandarin) or military service ; for these latter *compel* them to abuse
and maltreat the foreigner, whose free and enlightened intercourse
may very possibly interfere with their despotic and grossly tyrannical
rule.   We accompanied the rice-planters to their little village near
by, and here were entertained to tea and cakes ; and I must say that
during all my travels in various climes I never came across a more
genuine, courteous, hospitable people.   Only one event occurred
to make us feel the slightest superiority to these very interesting
people, and that was when, in the height of their friendship, and in
response to our curiosity, they deigned to initiate us into the
mysteries of " small foot," and caused one of their women to uncover
those hideous pedal deformities.   It was too dark to find our way
homeward when we bade adieu to our friends, so two of them very
kindly accompanied us as far as the beach with large paper lanterns.

We arrived on board only just in time to escape a good ducking ;

for, by the time that dinner was served, the rain was coming down in torrents, whilst the wind was whistling and howling through the schooner's cordage in a way that made us keep all snug below.

8 *p.m.*

"Rouse and bitt! rouse and bitt, my hearties!" roared old Jack Backstay, the moment that the sound was out of the bell. "Turn to here! Get into your places, light up your 'bacca, and keep a 'weather eye lifting,' for it's my turn to-night, and I'm just about to veer away my yarn."

We took our places, helped ourselves to toddy and cigars, or a cup of coffee if we preferred it, and then our entertainer for the night began his yarn, the elements seeming anxious to form an appropriate accompaniment to his opening scene—a shipwreck—for the bleak winds whistled, and roared, and howled outside, whilst the waves, though scarcely three feet deep, splashed and dashed in mimic fury against the immovable sides of the mud-embedded bark.

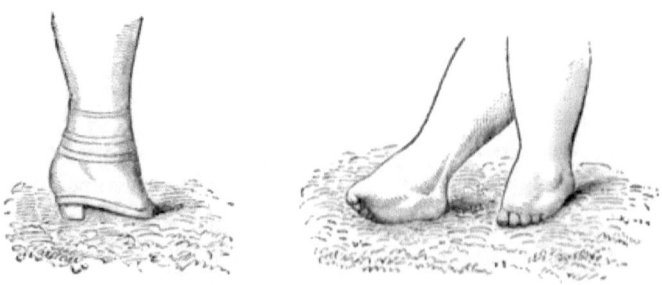

THE "SMALL FOOT," NAKED AND IN ITS SHOE.

CAUGHT BY CHINESE REBELS.

A STRANGE STORY OF CHINA.

THE third of December is a date indelibly impressed upon my memory, for, sixteen years ago, I was shipwrecked off the north-east coast of China upon that day of the month; moreover, I and Richard Savage, the second mate, were the only white men saved.

The fatal loss of the good ship *Shadow* and nearly her whole crew never became duly chronicled, from the simple circumstance that she was an illegal trader; being, in fact, one of those well-armed, clipper-built, opium smugglers, not exactly unknown in Chinese waters some years ago, before England had compelled the Imperial Celestial Government to legalise the wholesale importation of the pernicious drug grown in British India.

The *Shadow* was a smart little full-rigged ship of 400 tons burden—in fact, one of the smartest in the service. She carried a strong European crew, with a sufficient complement of Chinese sailors to man one boat (the natives being good oarsmen, and better able than white men to endure the fatigue of a long pull in the hot summer), besides other Celestials as servants, for which employment they are really admirably suitable. The rakish little *Shadow* was also fully equipped with an armament of twelve eighteen-pounders —six on either broadside—and a "long twenty-four," as pivot-gun amidships.   Many a time the heavy *Ti-Mungs* and Chinese war-junks found that we were quite able to fight our way, even when a dozen of them tried to effect our capture.   However, on the present occasion, I am not going to describe either the fighting exploits or substantial profits of the celebrated *Shadow*, but at once get to the subject of my story, and explain how Dick Savage, my servant, and myself fell into the hands of a large force of Chinese rebels.

About the end of November our vessel left Hong-Kong, half loaded with a valuable cargo of opium ; and the orders were to dispose of it at several small towns along the coast, between the former port and that of Swatow, some two hundred miles to the north and east.

We had been very successful at the first place to which we had been directed, and had landed more than a hundred chests of opium, for which our captain had received the hard cash, with a profit more than trebling the original outlay.   Then, getting under weigh, with a strong, fair wind, we sailed along the coast in search of the next port. The breeze continually increased, and, towards nine o'clock in the evening, we were dashing along at a distance of about three miles from the land, when all hands were startled by the loud and alarming cry from the look-out men stationed on the forecastle.   " Breakers ahead !   Hard a-port !" they shouted with terrible earnestness.

Too late !   They had seen the high ripple caused by the breaking of the rising sea over a sunken rock, upon which the next moment, before a rope could be touched, or a spoke of the wheel shifted, our doomed vessel crashed with terrific force.   Being built for speed, to attain which it is necessary to sacrifice strength, the *Shadow* was ·stove bodily in at once.   We had been dashing along before the gale at fully eleven knots an hour, when we went upon some unknown rock off Breaker Point—a projecting headland some sixty miles south of

Swatow—so the terrible force with which we struck may easily be imagined. Most of the crew were drowned in their hammocks; for, even as the masts came crashing over the side, the ship—having, I believe, run up the side of a sloping rock—heeled right over, and, with her hold already full of water, slipped off and sank.

Fortunately for me, though it was my watch below, I had been enjoying a cheroot, and building castles in the air, under the lee of the weather bulwarks amidships. When the ship struck, I was hurled right across the deck, striking with great violence against the carriage of the long gun. When I recovered myself she was sinking, and, amid falling spars, shouting men, dashing waves, and the terrible grind-grind, crash-crash of the poor old vessel's hull upon the rocks, I seized one of the life-buoys hanging to the poop-rail, and sprang overboard. I jumped to leeward, knowing well that if I took the other side I should either be drifted under the hull or get into the *chow-chow* water rushing and eddying around the rocks. Getting one of the bights of the lanyard over my head, and resting the edge of the buoy under my chin, I pushed it before me, nicely supporting myself in spite of the roughness of the sea, and striking out so vigorously that I scarcely felt the suction of the waters closing over the sinking ship.

I was not alone in my struggle for life. I felt a melancholy sort of satisfaction in knowing that. Every now and then the tossing waves would show me here and there a small dark object; and I knew these dots as the heads of others swimming for their lives. But then, alas! at short intervals, came, even above the howling of the gale, the "bubbling cry of some strong swimmer in his agony!" These fearful incidents would palsy my exertions for a time, during which I could not do more than cling despairingly to the life-buoy.

I was not much of a swimmer, so, after the first spurt, did not

K

make great progress towards the land.   One by one the heads of my
unfortunate companions disappeared, and I knew that I was alone—
alone on that raging sea!   Who can imagine the mental agony I
endured whilst clinging to that life-buoy?   Dashed hither and thither
by the black-looking, strangely-sparkling phosphorescent waves, what
an insignificant atom I became!   The frowning heavens, hanging low
with heavy, inky clouds, afforded not one ray of hope—one sign of
comfort.   Why or how could *I* be saved, when all my late companions
had been doomed to perish?   Alone on the angry waters!   Alone!
with no saving hand to help; no pitying heart to note my solitary
agony!   No. eye, save that of God, to witness my untimely death!   It
was terrible—terrible!   I know not how long a time had elapsed—
how long I had been struggling on, despair at my heart, and little
energy in my efforts—when suddenly I was startled and overjoyed at
the faint sound of a distant cry.   What could it be?   In a moment—
so tenacious of life are we frail mortals, and so easily aroused from the
depths of despair to the extreme altitude of hope—I threw off the
lethargic helplessness into which I had fallen, and shouted aloud with
my utmost strength.   How anxiously I strained my sense of hearing,
in order to distinguish above the whistling of the fierce wind any sound
that might come in reply!   I had not long to wait.   The echo of that
welcome voice came to me again, and I felt almost certain that it was
my faithful Indian servant crying—

"Malem Sahib! Malem Sahib!" (smallest sir, &c.)

This was my Indian title, for I was the junior officer (third mate)
of the late *Shadow*.   I knew that the cry proceeded from the faithful
Ali, he being the only native of the East Indies who had been on
board.   For seven years had he truly served me, and I almost considered him more an inseparable humble friend than a menial.   How I

should have done without him I know not. His services had become
indispensable to me; and many a time had he saved my life by
tenderly and carefully nursing me through fevers and epidemics that
had proved fatal to many of my brother officers not so well looked
after. When I left the Indian Navy and took to smuggling, Ali
accompanied me: he saved my life upon this occasion, after the loss
of the *Shadow*, and once again, as will be seen hereafter.

During a momentary lull of the gale I again heard him cry—

"Hoodah, Sahib! hoodah!" (Hold on, sir! hold on!) "hold on,
sare, leetle longer. I come. You sing out for me which way come."

Before long, up to me he came from out of the surrounding darkness and desolation, pushing a stun'-sail-boom end on before him, and
swimming wonderfully fast, considering the size of the spar. As for
me, I could not possibly have swum another hundred yards, and the
land was yet about two miles distant.

"Sare," said Ali, upon getting hold of me, and lashing me fast
to his spar with a bit of rope, "more bettah swim with me very jilti
(quick) fast. Burrah Malem Sahib (the second mate) have go try
to get ashore: he talk me have got tide set to Breaker Point. Spose
not jilti jow (quickly go) we no can catch it: tide take us go outside.
Ah! Bode ar-char, bode ar-char! I very too much glad to find you.
I long time burrah (great) fear you have die—have sink down, down,
to bottom of de sea!"

And the poor fellow, having been swimming about that wild sea
to find me, actually shed tears of joy at having done so, I believe.

His communication quite aroused me to the necessity of strenuous
exertion. The tide set up the coast, and, from about the position where
the *Shadow* went down, ran directly for Breaker Point. But then, as
it would be sure to sweep outward again round the Point, unless we

could manage to swim far enough inland to be carried ashore inside that
rocky extremity, we would surely be carried out to sea again and lost.

Ali, having lashed me fast to one end of the stun'-sail boom,

THE OLD FISHERMAN.

swam to the other; and then, making himself fast to it with a piece of
its lashing, proceeded to strike out vigorously for the shore, towing
me and the boom after him, though I did my utmost to help.

We passed through several tide-ripples, the thick spray from which, tossed by the high sea and driven by the strong gale, flew so densely over us that I became insensible at last, and must have very nearly died of suffocation.

Ali was a native of Madras, where the people are the most expert swimmers in the world, and he was consequently quite at his ease in the water, even in the roughest weather. He got me ashore somehow, for when I regained my senses it was to find myself lying on the mud floor of a miserable little fisher hut, whilst he was bending over me, chafing my hands and striving to pour a basin of scalding tea down my throat.

I soon recovered, and gazed around. The only other occupant of the wretched, one-roomed shanty was a wild-looking old Chinese fisherman; and his appearance, by the scanty, flickering light shed by a piece of pith burning in a cup of fish-oil, was strange, savage, and outlandish. That part of the head which the Chinese usually shave clean was covered with at least a couple of months' growth of hair several inches long, and sticking straight and bristly up all round; whilst his pig-tail, unplaited, was twisted loosely around his brawny throat. With the exception of loose petticoat trousers that had once been blue, but had now been washed out of any particular colour, and which were entirely composed of patches that hid the whole of the original stuff, this wild-looking fellow was perfectly naked. His face, arms, and chest, through constant exposure to the sun, the storm, and every kind of weather, had changed from the pale yellowish-brown Chinese complexion to the darkest tinge short of negro black. He sat watching us with astonishment, as well he might, considering how, through the raging storm, and over the angry sea, we had come drifting to his solitary beach. He spoke not; neither did he move. Only his oblique little black eyes sparkled in the flickering lamplight.

For some moments he sat thus motionless and regarding us. He had seen Ali drag me into his hut, and then take possession of his hot tea to pour down my throat, apparently with equal indifference. At length, however, when I had recovered sufficiently to stand up, we moved closer towards him, as the wind came whistling chilly through the large crevices of the rough door, near which I had been lying. No sooner had we left the entrance clear, than, with one swift bound, he sprang to his feet and dashed out of the place at a speed defying all pursuit. He had, no doubt, been so still and silent before through fear. From what I knew of Chinese character I felt pretty sure that he had taken us for a couple of real devils. He lived at a very lonely, out-of-the-way part of the coast, and most likely had never before seen either a white or a black man. No wonder that he felt superstitiously alarmed at the sudden and extraordinary first appearance before him of a specimen of each strange race.

We were sitting, laughing at the fright of our unwilling host, when our merriment ceased upon the appearance of some one in the open doorway. The next moment, my brother officer and particular friend, Dick Savage, staggered into the hut, and, sinking by my side in an exhausted state, hoarsely said—

"Thank God! Thank God, I am not alone!"

We sat silent for a moment, clasping each other by the right hand. Then I asked—

"How did you ever manage to reach the shore, Dick?"

"Heaven alone can tell! I swam it *somehow*," he replied. "But you? How did you get saved? You cannot swim nearly as well as I can, yet it was as much as ever I could do to reach the shore!"

I pointed to my black friend, and said—

"Ali saved me, or I should be with the rest of our unfortunate shipmates; for I fear that none besides ourselves have lived to tell the tale."

"None!" emphatically cried my chum, "for I got ashore at the other end of this bay, and have walked all round it to get here; but not a sign of them could I see, though, God knows! I looked anxiously enough about. Little did I think to have the joy of finding *you*, Jack, safe, and landed before me!"

And I have no doubt that our eyes became rather moister than usual, as we clasped hands again, feeling overjoyed at the escape of ourselves, but being deeply affected at the terribly sudden loss of all our other shipmates and companions.

Dick, however, was not of a disposition long to remain sentimental, and though, upon rubbing his eyes with the back of his hands, he pretended that it was the effect of the salt water made them so red and moist, he soon recovered his exuberant animal spirits, and proceeded to rummage about the hut in search of provisions, eventually bringing to light a small pan of cold boiled rice and *ditto* fish. No other eatables were in the place, and these were very soon warming at the little charcoal stove.

"I say," said he, suddenly, "suppose the Celestial owner of the shanty returns and finds us making ourselves at home? The coast people are particularly unscrupulous, and, if our unknown host should happen to return accompanied by his friends, the consequences might prove rather unpleasant to our humble selves!"

Hereupon I communicated to my friend the hasty disappearance of the old fisherman just before his own arrival. Upon describing the wild-looking fellow's appearance and alarm, I happened to mention the unshaved state of his head.

"What!" cried my friend, interrupting. "Unshaved, do you say? Well, then, all I can tell you is that we have got into a pretty place. We must be somewhere upon the territory occupied by the rebels—the 'Chung-maous' (*i.e.*, 'long-haired'). Those fellows, you know, do not shave the head; but let all their hair grow long, in opposition to the shaven and tail-wearing badge of subjection imposed by the Tartars when they conquered China some two hundred years ago. No doubt, as patriots, they have a perfect right to rebel against the tyrannical Tartar government, and adopt the old Chinese custom of wearing the hair; but then they are reported to be terribly cruel and remorseless. Shiver my timbers, Jack, I trust we shall not fall into their patriotic clutches!"

I had heard of this strange rebellion; an insurrection rapidly increasing. It was supposed to combine a religious element with its political aim, for the insurgents were sometimes spoken of as "God-worshippers," sometimes as "Chung-maous." As for the stories of their cruelty, I did not at all believe them, knowing well the unreliable and distorted nature of all Chinese reports. We were discussing the point, whilst finishing the fisherman's eatables, when the sound of voices outside at once arrested our attention.

Dick Savage having snatched up an old hatchet, I had just succeeded in making him give it up, and impressing upon his mind that implicit submission constituted our only chance to obtain good treatment from the natives, either rebels or Imperialists, when the door was opened, and in came—or rather, in was led—the old fisherman, accompanied by half-a-dozen of his countrymen.

Our host, *bon gré, mal gré*, trembled excessively as he once more faced, not two, but *three* supernatural visitors! Evidently he had been compelled to return and lead his present companions to those whom he had no doubt described in an extraordinary manner. Upon finding his hut in possession of three strange beings, when he had left it in the hands of only two, his superstitious fears were greatly increased, and it was as much as ever the others could do to prevent him breaking from their hold and running away again. Immediately on their arrival I recognised those who accompanied the fisherman as rebels. I knew it by their wild, dashing, independent, and highly picturesque appearance ; moreover, their glossy black tresses were growing long and uncut, being gathered together at the back of the head and plaited into a long, thick tail, interwoven with red silk cord, which formed a large tassel at the end. This was then wound round the head as a natural turban, the scarlet tassel hanging over the left shoulder. A more handsome and becoming head-dress it would have been impossible to imagine ; the heavy braids of raven hair and scarlet silk shading their swarthy, sunburnt countenances and glittering black eyes. Then their dress also was quite different to any Chinese costume I had previously seen. The leader of the party, a tall, noble-looking man, wore a crimson silk hood, ornamented with a pearl badge over the forehead, probably denoting his rank ; this style and colour admirably became his dark, intelligent features. He was clad in a short silken jacket, quilted throughout, and of the same crimson hue as the hood. The rest of the party, evidently the chief's attendants, wore their own hair for head-dress, as before described, and were variously clad in scarlet or blue jackets and extremely wide black or blue petticoat trousers. All were armed except the chief, whose sword was carried by one of the others. The arms consisted of bows and arrows, matchlocks, spears, and every one wore a short, thick sword.

Although, when this picturesque party appeared, Dick made a

wofully long face, and angrily muttered, " Caught by Chinese rebels !
just what I expected, by Jove ! I wonder how they'll eat us—roast or
boiled ? " *I* nevertheless was at once favourably impressed by them.
It was not altogether owing to their dashing manner and picturesque
appearance ; but I appreciated the fact that there seemed about them
an indescribable sort of moral elevation—an elevation and change of
character as distinct from, and superior to, that of the ordinary
Tartar-ruled Chinese I had hitherto encountered, as was their
becoming difference of costume.   Not long afterwards Dick became
infected with the same idea ; in fact, as will be seen, it produced a
greater impression upon him than upon myself.

Entering the hut, the chief advanced to where we were seated
by the little charcoal fire, shivering in our wet clothes ; and after
regarding us intently for a moment or two, saluted us by clasping his
hands and saying—

" Tsin tsin, yang ta-jin ? " (How do you do, foreign excel-
lencies ?)

" Hallo ! " cried Dick ; " why they don't seem so savage,
after all."

I understood a little Chinese, so returned the chief's salutation,
and, rising to my feet, politely begged him to take a seat.

The old fisherman—his fear giving way to curiosity—looked
rather wroth at this, as though he thought the strange devils cheeky,
anyhow, and then stepped forward to do the honours of his humble
abode himself ; politeness being quite a virtue with the interesting
natives of China—the most alarming events seldom making them
forget its practice.   My breach of etiquette, having aroused the old
fellow's breeding, quite dissipated his fears.   The most ignorant
Chinaman knows how to be polite, and civility seems natural to him,

THE REBEL CHIEF.

when not corrupted by the proximity of Chinese *braves* or Tartar soldiers.

The chief then, according to etiquette, inquired as to our names and native place. I informed him; and when I told him how we had been wrecked, and how providentially we had managed to reach the shore, he expressed great pity and astonishment. He at once gave orders for two of his attendants to run back to their camp and take a party of men with torches to search along the beach for any more survivors of the wreck. But what surprised me more than all, instead of attributing our deliverance to poor dumb, wooden idol " Joss," as the ordinary Chinese would have done, he said that " Tien voo," *i.e.*, " The Heavenly Father," had saved us. I now understood how it was the rebels had received the name of " God-worshippers." No doubt there was a strong religious element in the movement, and, at all events, the chief seemed to recognise the one true God, whereas his Imperialist countrymen were all either Confucionists or Buddhists. When, in my turn, I asked his name, native place, and employment, he informed me that his name was Le, that he came from the province of Kwang-si, and was now a chieftain in the army of " God-worshippers," lying encamped a mile or so inland. He now begged that we would accompany him thither; which we were nothing loth to do, being wet, cold, and very miserable in our present wretched quarters. We were also greatly pleased at being addressed as " Foreign brothers " (" Yang-te "), whereas nearly all Chinese term foreigners " Foreign devils " (" Yang quitzos ").

Upon reaching the camp, we were so tired that the chief allowed us to retire at once, he having provided us with dry Chinese clothes, warm rugs, and sleeping quarters in a tent close by his own.

" Well," said Dick, " before we go to sleep, I must say that chief

is a capital fellow—not a bit Chinese in appearance or behaviour.   I
like these rebels.   Confound the lubberly swabs who run them down !
' Cruel murderers,' ' bloodthirsty brigands,' indeed !   They are far
better men than those who term them so.   What do you say,
Jack ? "

I readily assented, being convinced that the insurrectionists were
far superior, both physically and intellectually, to the rest of their
countrymen.   I could only account for this very extraordinary change
by supposing it to be the ennobling effect of their determined break
from the degrading systems of idolatry and slavery to which the
Chinese people have so long been subjected.   In the morning, the
first thing that we did was to climb over a neighbouring ridge of rock,
ascend a lofty eminence, and gaze forth upon the scene of the previous
night's disaster.   The bay at which we had managed to get ashore
lay fully revealed before us, and a dreary, bleak, desolate, and yet
wildly picturesque, scene it was.

Not a sign or vestige of either the wreck or our late comrades
could we see, so we decided to have a nearer inspection of the beach
before leaving that part.   Just then we were astonished by the loud
sound of prayer coming from the direction of the camp, so turned
back to it, and then saw a sight that I shall never forget.

The army was camped upon a large plain, and now the whole
extent of level ground was covered with a vast multitude on their
knees in prayer.   The leader and originator of this wonderful movement was standing upon a slightly elevated platform, reading from
what I ascertained to be a Chinese translation of the Bible.   He
was a tall, handsome man, in the prime of life, with regular, almost
European, features, an extremely massive brow, and an eye of fire.
He was something more than a remarkable native ; he would have

THE BAY.

been a distinguished and leading man in any country. His whole appearance presented an indescribable nobleness and dignity. His presence was imposing and commanding. His loud, sonorous, and melodious voice penetrated far over that wide-stretching plain, and the eloquent words seemed to thrill to the heart of every kneeling follower. The chief evidently possessed a mighty power over the varied host at his feet. I saw, in a moment, that his will was theirs; that an intense enthusiasm, made up of excited patriotism and religious fervour, pervaded the whole multitude; and that all as one man eagerly fulfilled his slightest behest. This extraordinary man, already clad in the yellow imperial robes, denoting his own ambition and the wish of his followers to plant him upon the throne in place of the present usurping Tartar occupant, was Hung-Sui-tshuen, the leader and originator of the rebellion, and who, later, upon the capture of Nankin and many other important places, became known to Europeans as the *Tien Wang—i.e.,* Heavenly King—the king and high priest of the great Taiping revolution.

As I gazed forth upon that kneeling multitude, athwart whose upturned faces the early morning sun now cast aslant its golden rays of glory, I felt that the hand of God was plainly visible in the remarkable sight before me. How, otherwise, could these thousands and tens of thousands have arisen from their depths of heathenism and degradation? The ancient and mystic lore—the deeply-venerated teaching of the deified sages of China—followed and implicitly believed for upwards of two thousand years—had been cast aside, and this regenerating host now bent the knee so devoutly in the Christian faith and worship of the true God.

As we looked forth from our tent, and stood dumb with astonishment at the strange scene, the multitude rose up from their knees,

I.

A FEMALE REBEL OFFICER.

and, in obedience to the gesture of their leader, every voice was lifted up in a simple hymn of praise and supplication. So strange and foreboding a sight had never before been witnessed in that ancient and exclusive country, and it promised hope for arousing the vast Chinese population from the state of moral lethargy in which they had so long been sunk. Altogether, an extraordinary psychological phenomenon was before us. That varied host contained men, boys, women, girls, children, and venerable persons hanging for support on the arms of their younger relatives. They were of every rank and

THE LAST SEARCH FOR TRACES OF THE WRECK.

grade, from the poor *coolie* to him who had been a wealthy mandarin; and all alike, both man, woman, and child, seemed imbued with the same religious fervour and patriotic enthusiasm. Many of the women were armed, and they were all formed into regular sections of twenty-five, under a female officer. Many of these female officers were young and handsome women; but now the softer feelings, the coquetry, and the more frivolous occupations of the sex, seemed given up and abandoned for the stern realities of war. The women were all kept apart from the men in separate camps, and their higher officers were (at this place) lodged in a solitary Confucian temple, at the door of which one of them kept guard, spear in hand. The men were all employed as soldiers, and were formed in very uneven regiments

under their respective officers.   Weapons were rough and scarce,
the drilling evidently imperfect; but the strictest discipline prevailed,
and this, no doubt, together with their great enthusiasm, gave the
insurgents that surprising superiority over the Imperialist troops
which had ensured them the victory in every encounter.   The
infinite variety of their military costume, chosen of the brightest
and most gorgeous colours; the rich floating folds of the innumerable
silken banners streaming on the wind; the grandeur, the solemn
grandeur, of those myriad voices echoing back with prolonged reverberation from the high crests of the neighbouring mountains; the
whole variegated appearance of the multitude of well and becomingly-
dressed members of a new people, as it were, united for the cause
of freedom, and even more united in the fixed determination to
Christianise their mighty empire—these facts presented a grand and
wonderfully imposing moral aspect.

I had heard of this wonderful movement.   How its leader had
singularly met with a copy of the Scriptures translated into Chinese;
how he had been himself converted by it, and then imagined that he
had a divine commission to convert his countrymen; how, also,
upon meeting with extraordinary success, his congregation of " God-
worshippers" had taken up arms in consequence of the cruel perse-
cutions to which the mandarins had subjected them ; but little did I
dream what a mighty movement had been set on foot.   Even as we were
still gazing upon the strange scene, bewildered with the singular change
from our terrible shipwreck on the previous evening, the prayers
came to a conclusion—the mighty voice of that vast concourse of
upwards of one hundred thousand persons became silent, save where
the officers gave their sharp commands, as the whole army prepared
to strike its tents and march.

At this moment a party of soldiers came to furl our tent and take it with the rest, and I accompanied them to the division commanded by our friend the chieftain, Le; whilst my companion, getting a pipe and some tobacco, took a last and solitary walk along the beach, without, however, finding any trace whatever of the wreck.

All day long the march was continued without a single halt, and I became aware that a large Imperialist army was following close in pursuit. At length, towards dusk, the course of a swollen river delayed our march until the vanguard of the pursuers came in sight The commander of the rebels now pushed forward with the main body of his followers, convoying baggage, women, and non-combatants, and leaving General Le with a rearguard to dispute the passage of the river as long as possible.

We had marched far inland, and the formation of the country was mountainous, the river, for many miles both above and below the crossing, flowing between steep rocky banks. Though elsewhere the breadth of the stream was rather insignificant, yet at the point to which, on either side, the low land descended and the beaten roads converged, it spread out into lake-like fulness, and was studded with numerous heavily-wooded islets; whilst here and there, just showing above the surface of the water, some glittering sand-banks attested that the generally deep channel had become shallow in proportion to its increased breadth.

On these low islands, and the shore to which his retreating friends had crossed, Le posted his men, and prepared to resist the enemy; and, somehow, having remained with him, we made up our minds to assist him; a sort of Anglo-Saxon pride preventing us watch the preparations for the coming fight as non-combatants.

Contrary to usual Chinese tactics (which consist in making a manifold greater display than the real force justifies) our chief masked every position, and placed his men in perfect concealment.

When the Imperialists reached the large military station on the opposite side of the river, they found that we (as we joined in their proceedings, I suppose that Dick, Ali, and myself, were entitled to speak of the rebel "God-worshippers" as "we"); well, then, the enemy, found that we had not only *looted* their station, but had also very wisely carried off all the gun-boats and other craft. The pursuit was, therefore, arrested until some means of crossing could be obtained. We could see parties of cavalry setting off both up and down the bank, probably to bring in any boats that might be found. Meanwhile other detachments of the enemy were busily at work constructing rafts.

On the following day a strong squadron of gun-boats arrived from some neighbouring station. These vessels are about forty feet long, six or seven wide, very shallow, and pull from ten to twenty oars a side ; carrying, also, a mast (or two) and sail, a couple of six or twelve-pounder guns (one in the bow, the other in the stern), and a crew of from twenty-five to fifty men. They constitute an effective and formidable musquito flotilla on the lakes, rivers, and innumerable canals of China.

After a very cursory reconnoitre of our shore, the Imperialists made preparations to effect the crossing ; being, no doubt, deceived by our silence and secrecy, and believing that the passage would not be disputed. It was quite dusk when the rafts were finished, and then a small squadron of gun-boats came over to our side of the river in order to protect the intended landing-place. As nothing could be seen of the rebels, the crews—with true Chinese apathy—spread their awnings fore and aft, boiled their evening rice, and then resigned themselves to

OUR POSITION ON THE RIVER.

sleep, leaving a man to keep the gong going in the bow of each vessel; as for keeping any *look-out*, that seemed to be the last thought of the mariners on watch, their entire energy being divided between snatching the regular intervals of slumber which they had accustomed themselves to enjoy when on duty, and mechanically starting up to make a noise by striking one clanging blow on the gong, following it up by two strokes in rapid succession, and then to sleep again. Little did they dream how very closely they were being watched!

Gradually the misty vapours, blending with the shades of night, formed a thick haze over the surface of the water; the heavily-wooded islets, as well as the further shore, becoming perfectly hidden from the Imperialist encampment. At something like hourly intervals, however, the faint *klang-ng-ng, klang-klang* of the gongs on board the advanced squadron could be heard; between while *quack, quack, quack* went the countless flocks of wild-fowl; and these sounds, mingling with the melancholy note of the solitary bittern, the peculiar cry of the startled curlew, and the heavy, humming noise of the busy nocturnal insects, continued till the dawn of day. No change was noticed by the Imperialist sentinels and patrols; no suspicion of danger was entertained by the drowsy watchmen of the distant gun-boats.

Towards midnight, however, great flocks of the wild birds flew screaming from their favourite haunts among the islands of the river, and the solitary creeks, inlets, and lagoons of the shore to which the retreating host had crossed. It would have required keen eyes in close proximity to have distinguished the shadowy human forms stealing forward through the thick mist and heavy darkness resting upon the dense vegetation of the islets and the neighbouring land. From out numberless natural hiding-places, where little streams slowly flowed in silence and in solitude beneath umbrageous canopies of spreading foliage and weeping-willow, a good many tiny boats or punts (such as are used all over China by the numerous keepers of the vast flocks of tame ducks) were gently paddled to an appointed rendezvous at the largest islet, where the chief, Le, had established his head-quarters. From this position the distance was but short to where the enemy's out-lying vessels were stationed off the river's bank.

Klang-ng-ng, klang-klang, sonorously reverberated the gongs. Then all became silent again. At length, when half the time to the striking of the next hour had fled, several dark little objects might have been discerned hovering near the Imperialist squadron, but so small and undistinguishable from the surrounding darkness, that, even had the sleepy watchmen happened to notice them, they would most likely have taken them for wild geese or swans sleeping on the surface of the water. These little objects soon drifted away.

Soon afterwards the rebel chief received the report of his scouts, several punts having returned with information.

It was almost time to beat the gong again, but the dozing watch-men started up only to find themselves in our hands. A loud voice called upon them to surrender or die, and they chose the former with unanimous and truly Celestial apathetic equanimity. With muffled oars and rowlocks we had come down upon the enemy with the gun-boats that had been captured at the station, and by which the insurgent host had crossed the river.

Within five minutes the outlying squadron was towed off to the secret places among the islands.

Great must have been the astonishment of the Tartar general and his army when daylight made them aware of the disappearance of their friends. Several gun-boats were at once sent off to ascertain whether they were lying behind the islands. The detachment proceeded on its mission, but did not return. We were on the alert, and, no sooner had the explorers become hidden by the islands that they left between themselves and their position on the opposite shore, than we suddenly pounced upon them from our places of concealment, and captured them without encountering more than a momentary show of resistance. The enemy waited patiently for several hours, but then, finding that the second squadron neither returned nor replied to their signal-guns, began to suspect our rebellious presence, and made ready to explore the islands with their whole flotilla.

In the meanwhile our host and General was busy with his men constructing three new batteries, and mounting them with cannon taken from some of the prizes. We heartily assisted; and, from my knowledge of gunnery, I was enabled to be of some service, as I induced the chief to plant one battery in front, on the principal island, and one on either flank, so as to give a powerful cross-fire. The Chinese know that Europeans are better gunners than they can pretend to be, and Le, *ta-jin*, at once installed us as his principal artillerists. Dick remained ashore with the largest battery, whilst I and my faithful Ali proceeded on board the best-armed gun-boat.

At last the Imperialists began to advance, and a gallant sight they made, each of their vessels being profusely decorated with gaudy flags, and being filled with fully accoutred troops. Blowing their strange, melancholy-sounding war-horns, and keeping up a tremendous crash of gongs and Tartar drums, they rowed forward in close order. On they came, faster and faster, more daring and fearless as no sign of foe could be detected, until within a hundred yards of the largest islet, when suddenly, as if by magic, the artificial screens of cut boughs were thrown aside, and the three batteries opened a steady, well-directed cannonade, whilst all the captured gun-boats were pulled to the most commanding situations to take part in the conflict, and every bush seemed alive with an armed man. Though taken by surprise, the Imperialists gallantly replied to our fire, and still endeavoured to advance.

Startled and scared from their most secluded retreats, the affrighted wild-fowl hurried to and fro amongst the rank growth of sedge and osier. Occasionally some curious or daring bird would paddle its way to the margin of the rushes, in which case the flash of the artillery, and the sight of the battle array, always made it fly shrieking away. The timid fish rose in alarm to the surface only to dive deeper than ever to the lowest recesses of the river's bed; but their more ravenous brethren glided eagerly about in the neighbourhood of the battle, swimming as watchful and expectantly as the great carrion birds were waiting on the nearest trees, or soaring and circling high o'erhead. These things of prey had not long to wait, for the mangled bodies of Imperial soldiers, slain by our cannonade, were callously tossed overboard by their comrades, and sent drifting away with the current; and soon the savage birds and fishes were fighting as desperately over the bleeding carcases as the living men were striving their utmost to increase the number.

I can think of all this now, but at the time it seemed more like a dream. Only a day or two before, we had formed part of the *Shadow's* crew, and now!—now we were fighting against the Imperial Chinese troops, and serving in the ranks of the extraordinary rebels known as "God-worshippers!" We had no time to mourn for our lost shipmates; had it not been for the fatigue and bruises we still felt, the shipwreck would have seemed an event of the far past.

I can think of the incidents of the fight, and the change it caused on the face of nature, now, at this distant period; but during the engagement I became very seriously occupied in a desperate hand-to-hand encounter with one of the Imperial gun-boats.

One of our smallest craft had been sent with a message to the battery on the left flank of our position. This was on the main land, and all our gun-boats were concentrated higher up the river, between the central and right batteries. Having observed the departure of our despatch boat, one of the enemy's largest galleys had managed to follow in pursuit without exciting our attention, in consequence of the clouds of sulphurous smoke having just then drifted so as to obscure our view in that direction. When the wind happened to shift a little, we were infuriated to witness the fate of the small boat's crew. These unfortunates, being unable to escape from the galley which had followed them, seemed to have laid down their arms and surrendered. The smoke cleared from that direction just as the enemy's craft had run alongside. What was our horror and indignation when we saw the captors set upon and cruelly butcher their unfortunate prisoners! Forcing the necks of these wretched men upon the gunnel of the boat, the Imperialist *braves* barbarously hacked off their heads, leisurely inflicting the most horrible wounds, and effecting the decapitation by slowly sawing backwards and forwards with their knives. This was right in sight of our chief, who at once ordered the vessel I was on board to go round the back of one of the islands and try to cut off the bloodthirsty monsters from their friends.

The cruel sight had fairly raised my passions, and I felt as savage against the cruel enemy as did any of my rebel companions. Whilst they were pulling round the back of several islets, with the help of Ali I proceeded to carefully load the bow-gun (a foreign-made nine-pounder) with a heavy charge of grape and canister. By the time I had finished, and stood ready, match in hand, our boat had reached the extreme end of an island a little above where the enemy's galley was lying. Pulling close under cover of the bushes, we held on to the bank a moment, and then several of us stepped ashore to peer through the foliage and reconnoitre the position of the Imperialists before making a dash at them. The gun-boat was not fifty yards from where we lay, and we saw that the massacre was over, as she was towing the captured vessel astern, whilst all round the sides of the latter the gory heads of her unfortunate crew were sticking up on the ends of spears. In obedience to the low order of the captain of our galley, those who had crept ashore returned to their stations. The oars were doubly manned, and then, pushing off from the shore, we dashed upon the enemy, as our leader, standing up in the stern-sheets, waved his sword and cried, "Shang! shang!" (Forward! forward!)

Straining every nerve, our stalwart rowers made their tough oars bend like reeds, and the boat sprang forward through the water like a thing of life.

"Tah paou! tah paou!" (Fire the gun, &c.) roared the rebel captain.

I took a steady aim, Ali levered the black-looking muzzle just an inch or two to the right, then down went the burning match, and, even as the loud roar awoke repeated echoes among the woody islands, we could hear the dull *thud* of the grape, and the *patter patter* of the canister shot, taking effect on the adverse galley. Half a dozen of her men went down beneath the tempest of *mitraille*, the rest were too confused by our sudden appearance and effective fire to cut adrift their prize and get out of our way. Dropping their oars, most of them snatched up their arms to repel our attack, instead of pulling their vessel round and returning our fire. Giving one more vigorous pull altogether, which sent our galley stem on to the enemy's broadside, our crew then left their oars, took up their weapons, and, with a loud yell or cheer, we were upon the butchers of our comrades.

Matchlocks were fired, arrows whistled, spear-thrusts and sword-cuts were fiercely exchanged, and, after recovering from the shock with which we ran into them, the Imperial *braves* made desperate efforts to board us. During the *mêlée*, as the vessels drifted side by side, we saw the reason of their attempt. The force with which we had run into them had stove in portions of their hull below the surface, and their craft was rapidly filling with water. In spite of their loss from the discharge of our bow-gun, the enemy were still more numerous than ourselves, and we had to fight hard in order to keep them off. It was a regular hand-to-hand combat, nearly every man having one or more assailants. Somehow, I became engaged with the petty mandarin commanding the enemy. He was a tall, powerful fellow, and, no doubt, according to Chinese practice, a good swords-man. The boats were lying locked with their gunnels close together, so that we fought over the low sides, only a foot and a half high. My antagonist was armed with one of the straight and heavy Tartar cavalry swords, whilst I had a still more awkward Chinese-made blade. But for this, I could soon have ended the contest, for I had the reputation of being one of the best swordsmen in the Indian navy. My enemy was a strong fellow, and rained his blows both quick and heavy, still he could not touch me; but then my sword was so wretchedly made and clumsy a contrivance that I could not possibly handle it quick enough to take advantage of the many openings he gave me.

This resultless combat had been going on for some time—in silence on my part, though the mandarin kept encouraging himself and his *braves* by yelling, " Tah ! tah ! " (Fight ! fight !) and abusing me by shouting at me, " Sar, yang-quitzo ! " (Kill the foreign devil !)

At length, however, a savage-looking *brave* stepped to the side of his officer, and, bringing down his bamboo spear to the charge, prepared to impale me. The mandarin, encouraged at this, pressed me harder, and I could not give any attention to my new assailant. Another instant, and his spear would have been through me, when the faithful Ali came springing to my assistance.

With the marvellous rapidity of thought that sometimes takes place at such moments of extreme peril, I was just impressed with a confused sort of lightning-like panorama of my past life—I saw a dear fair face at home in England, and thought what a fool I was to get killed by mixing myself in the battles of the strange Chinese rebels—when Ali saved my life, and, alas ! poor fellow, lost his own in doing so.

He had already received a severe wound on the forehead, and I cannot tell whether or not he was half blinded with the blood flowing into his eyes ; but, unfortunately, instead of attacking the *brave*, he paid all his attention to the mandarin. Whirling aloft the short halbert he carried, he buried the axe-like blade in the brain of my immediate antagonist, but at the same instant was himself run through the heart by the spear-thrust intended for me. Before the *brave* could withdraw his weapon or move from the spot, the point of my sword had passed out at his back, and Ali was avenged.

I sprang back to the centre of our boat, and lifting the prostrate form of my faithful servant, was just in time to catch his dying sob. He opened his glazing eyes, and with difficulty said—

" Oh, Sahib ! master safe ?   I no care ; Bhudda talk die, I can't stop. Sahib, no let Chinaman put me—grave—lose caste. Don't forget me, Sahib——"

He was dead.

I imagine the fight only lasted another moment or two. We were victorious, completely so. The unfortunate boat's crew of captured and murdered rebels had been amply avenged; the Imperialist galley, with every soul on board, had been destroyed, and rested at the bottom of the river. The "God-worshippers" congratulated themselves, but *I*—I mourned for the death of my faithful companion and servant. This sad event, together with the vivid feeling that came over me in the moment of peril, and left behind a strong impression as to the folly of getting killed in a Chinese quarrel, and losing for ever that loved one in the old country, made me determine to leave the insurgents at the first opportunity, though I liked and admired them considerably.

Upon getting back to General Le's position, the battle had ceased, the enemy having been beaten off with heavy loss. The fearful hurtling noise and crashing of the deadly missiles, the terrible roar, and glare, and sulphurous smoke of battle no longer made the beautiful earth seem hideous. The waving flags no longer fluttered in defiance; the dissonant clanging of gong, the hollow beating of drum, and the dismal blast of war-horn had died away; the heavy bank of smoke was fast fading in the distance; the never-ceasing waters still flowed on, but the bright surface was no more broken by the splash and eddying ripple rising up from where the mangled remains of poor mortality had sunk. The birds became reassured, and flew merrily back to sing to the beauties of a splendid afternoon. The little fish again began to leap and play; their finny foes had ceased to chase and devour them; they were otherwise engaged.

M

All nature seemed to rejoice at the cessation of strife, and put forth its utmost charms to shame the murderous ferocity of man.

That evening, having received despatches from his leader, whose forces had captured and entered the city of Swatow without encountering any resistance, our chief silently abandoned his position and rejoined the main body.

The chieftain's wife was a charming person—most unusually well-informed and intelligent for a Chinese woman. She was very kind to us, and did all in her power to make us as comfortable as circumstances would permit. She shared in all the dangers of the fight, and was to be seen by her husband's side, in command of a female regiment, during the fiercest of the engagement. She was, fortunately for our native friend, as good a wife as Amazon; she rejoiced in the euphonious name of the Princess Wan-mei, and was very good-looking for a member of the great Mongolian family.

I carried—or rather, with the help of my friend Dick, carried—the body of poor Ali, and took care to observe his last request, that no Chinaman should touch him, and thereby, even in death, cause him to lose the caste to which he belonged. Though we supported the lifeless clay upon a sort of hammock slung to a couple of bamboo spears, it was hard work to reach Swatow with the burden; and though we Europeans may laugh at the East Indian's bigoted superstitions of caste, I could not do less for one who had so faithfully served me for so many years; who had several times saved my life; and who, at last, had sacrificed his own for mine. On Double Island (the foreign settlement at the port of Swatow) the remains of poor Ali were consigned to their last resting-place, in that corner of the cemetery appropriated to natives of India. Poor Ali! I could only raise a roughly-carved block of wood to his memory.

PRINCESS WAN-MEI.

Swatow was a port of considerable trade, and off Double Island some nine or ten European ships were riding at anchor. Taking leave of the chief, Le, I proceeded on board one of these vessels, meeting with a very kind reception from her officers upon making known the wreck of the *Shadow* and my own distressed circumstances.

My old chum accompanied me to the hospitable ship, but only to obtain some good arms, necessary clothing, and various useful things, such as a small compass, a telescope, medicines, &c., for he had determined to remain with the rebels and cast his fortune with theirs. Dick had become even more favourably impressed by them than I. If it had not been for the vivid recollections of my darling Fanny, whom I hoped to claim as my wife upon returning to England within a year, I should certainly have yielded to the earnest solicitations of the gallant chieftain, Le, and so have joined him with my friend. However, I bade Dick a lingering adieu ; he tore himself away with a parting wrench of the hand, and we never met again. In due course of time I visited home and claimed my bride. Once again, six years later, I made my last voyage to China. Then I found that Dick Savage was well known as a favourite general of the celebrated *Chung Wong*, *i.e.*, the Faithful Prince—Le, the Commander-in-Chief of the Taiping armies. At this time the revolution had wonderfully increased, and had wrested some of the fairest and richest provinces from the sway of the Manchoo-Tartar Government. The name of "God-worshippers" had been changed to "Taiping." Hung-Sui-tshuen, the leader and originator of the movement—he whom I had seen preaching to his followers the morning after my shipwreck—had been crowned Emperor of China, with the title of *Tien Wong ;* his government and capital was established at the

great and ancient city of Nankin ; the style and title adopted for the
new Chinese dynasty being *Tai ping tien kwoh*, *i.e.*, The Celestial
Kingdom of Universal Peace. These facts are notorious, and show
the grand projects, as well as the vast designs, which speedily
unfolded themselves to the mind of the extraordinary leader.
Nothing but an expulsion of the hated Tartar tyrants, the subversion
of the idolatrous system, and the incorporation of the whole nation
into one empire of " Universal Peace," as believers in the one true
God and Saviour, with the *Tien Wong* himself as political head and
religious chief of the whole, could henceforth satisfy the victorious
insurgents, inflamed by enthusiasm and animated by past success.
The strange history of that remarkable religio-political movement is
now pretty well familiar to the world. From what I personally saw
of the rebels I am convinced that they would have proved the
regenerators of their country, if let alone by foreign powers.

There is nothing more to relate. I have told how we were
caught by Chinese rebels. Dick became a famous general among
them ; but I, for my own part, prefer Fan and our comfortable little
English home to all the rebels in the world.

SWATOW.

THE LOG.

January 13th—One bell, 1h: 30m. a.m., had struck.

Concluding his yarn with a sigh of relief, Old Jack Backstay lugged forth a large golden locket from some secret recess near his heart, held it off admiringly for a moment at arm's length, and then pressed it to his lips with a hearty, ringing kiss. Of course, our curiosity being raised, we all had to have a look at his treasure, when a charming English face was revealed, and we all united in wishing our sturdy mariner a safe and speedy return to the arms of his loving Fan. A motion was proposed, and carried with unanimous acclamation, that our friend had spun the best and longest yarn—for it was of strange historical events even at this time in full course of action in that singular, interesting, vast, and little-known country where we all met together.

My idea of story-telling had proved a decided success ; so much so, indeed, that not one of us regretted having lost the proposed cruise by sticking in the mud ; and then our days were pleasantly passed in shooting, fishing, and rambling about the wild and beautiful scenery of the coast off which we had grounded—an occupation that also kept the " Angel " fully employed in working out various grilled, broiled, and roasted results, with a cunning and ingenuity peculiar to himself.

By this time my health and strength seemed fully restored—thanks to the change from that sultry, low-lying, unhealthy Shanghai, to the fresh, invigorating sea-air, and our enlivening ways and means *pour tuer le temps.*

7h. a.m.

Six bells struck this morning as we assembled on deck to have our usual bath. This delightful operation consisted in being douched with many buckets of sea-water; after which, like young horses, we were each vigorously rubbed down by a couple of sturdy Chinese tars, and our day began.

Again were our *un*trusty mariners employed in trying to heave the *Fortuna* off the mud-bank; but, although the rising tide nearly floated us, it fell again so soon, that their efforts were futile, and we remained in our old quarters.

After breakfast we all went ashore for another exploring excursion, and pulled a considerable distance along the coast to find a new landing-place. Instead, however, of doing this, we came upon the entrance to a large creek, of wild and picturesque appearance, as shown by the accompanying sketch.

Those big boots of mine came in very handy, except on this occasion. All around, about, and inside the mouth of the creek were numerous banks, some of mud, others of sand. These, naturally enough, formed the feeding-ground and resting-place to numerous flocks of wild-fowl. Getting a good shot at a covey of teal, I knocked several over, and they fell about the middle of one of these shoals. When the boat grounded I got out, depending upon my long boots to keep my feet dry, and went to pick up the birds. For the first few yards I went forward pretty well, but then each step I took went deeper; and, foolishly enough, I persisted in going on, until at length, when about half-way between the boat and the birds,

MOUTH OF THE CREEK.

I could neither advance nor return, whilst every moment saw me sink deeper and deeper in the treacherous soil. I then, for the first time, thoroughly experienced the extraordinary tenacity of Chinese mud— all the rivers, creeks, bays, and lagoons along the coast of the country are full of it. The more I struggled to get clear and return, the deeper I sank; when I was down to my knees I called to my friends for help. As I floundered about I lost my balance, and fell into the mud, becoming covered, as Esmond afterwards related to an admiring audience at Shanghai, from "clue to earing." At last the tops of my boots went below the surface and filled; and it was only after I had fastened the end of a rope (flung to me from the boat) around my waist, that my friends succeeded in extricating me from my particularly unenviable position and imminent risk of suffocation, and dragging me bodily through the mud on board. The boots were left behind; but the next morning an adventurous fisherman brought them on board—not altogether out of purely philanthropic motives, I venture to opine.

As it was too far to return on board the schooner for dry clothes, my comrades supplied me with various articles of attire until my own became sufficiently dry by hanging in the sun.

Meanwhile, our Chinese boatmen pulled away up the creek, which, in some places, became deep and narrow, between rocky banks, the land on either side being covered with a splendidly luxuriant mass of tropical vegetation.

We enjoyed ourselves very much in rambling about the beautiful scenery of this neighbourhood, and still kept pulling forward up the creek; now bumping upon shoals when it spread out broad and shallow at a part where the land was low and marshy, then narrowing to a deep and rapid course, with a rocky channel, below precipitous and overhanging banks; and then, anon, flowing silently and darkly beneath the umbrageous canopy of rustling, overarching foliage covering it in from side to side, and which sometimes hung so low upon the shaded waters that we had a difficulty in forcing our little *sanpan* through.

Our perseverance was at length well rewarded. After forcing our way along the creek for nearly an hour, we suddenly emerged upon the bosom of a magnificent river. It was not so much the stream itself—which was little more than half a mile broad, though very deep—as the grand and rugged scenery upon its banks that we admired. We sailed about for some little time, sometimes in the shadow of huge, towering masses of gigantic basalt cliffs, rising sheer from the river's edge to a height of many hundred feet, and darkly imprisoning its rock-bound channel between their stupendous sides.

We found but few signs of habitation along the margin of this beautiful stream, but, at one of the few little huts we came across, ascertained that it was the river Yu-yaou, which runs into, or is a branch of, the Fung-wha river, just where the city of Ningpo is built. It is true, the banks of the Yu-yaou seemed rocky and sterile, and this may account for its absence of population. Besides, it is not navigable to the sea, whilst the other branches of the Ningpo river which are, are thickly dotted all along their course with numerous towns and villages.

At noon we left the Yu-yaou, and, by way of the creek, returned on board. After tiffin, as the rest of our friends preferred remaining on board, Esmond and I took the ship's boat, and went out for some deep-sea fishing at a famously good spot a mile or so to seaward.

Here we had rare success, and in a short time nearly filled the stern-sheets of the boat with the captured fish. As, however, we had

THE RIVER YU-YAOU.

lost several lines, snapped with the greatest ease by some strange monsters of the deep, our curiosity and indignation became aroused, and we determined to catch and do to death some one or more of these formidable creatures. Taking a coil of two and a half inch rope, we fixed to it our largest hook, baited it with a large and tempting lump of pork fat, then tossed it over the side, awaiting the result in a fiendish sort of glee. We had not long to wait. There was suddenly a tremendous tug.

" Hooked him, by Jupiter ! " roared Esmond.

Then up he hauled a huge sea-bream, nearly as big as himself, and which he had the utmost difficulty to get on board, whilst I laid on the opposite gunnel, to keep the boat from capsising.

The period at which our last yarn was to be commenced (for we knew that the morrow's tide would set us afloat) found myself and friends all gathered together round the cuddy-stove as usual.

The " Angel " bustled about with bottles of his master's very best strong waters ; the manillas were produced ; and, in addition, a small box of rare old havanas—never brought out except on grand occasions. A supper of unusual magnificence engaged our servants in its preparation ; extra lamps were lighted—in fact, everything that could either be thought of or obtained to add to our comfort and celebrate a special event was forthcoming ; but then, it was the anniversary of the stanch *Fortuna's* launch, which came but once a year, and our host was fond of making holiday ; therefore, let us eat, drink, yarn, and be merry.

At least ten minutes before the appointed hour my friends had proceeded to establish themselves in their accustomed places. Then I ascertained that they were impatient to hear my yarn, for I had previously informed them that it would be the narration of an important

N

episode in my own life; through which, indeed, was to be indirectly attributed my present trip to the East, and consequent acquaintance with themselves, only excepting Esmond, who had been a brother officer of mine during two different voyages.

8h. p.m.

No sooner had the echo of the *Fortuna's* silvery bell died away, than I took the chair, " spliced the main-brace " (with some of the skipper's best brew), and began to spin my own yarn.

OUR FISHING.

THE BLACK PIRATE.

A TALE OF THE SEA.

"COME, Mister Mainstay," cried our captain, anxiously, "what do you make of her?"

"Well, sir," replied the chief officer, emphatically, lowering the spy-glass through which he had been gazing so long and deliberately as to make his superior impatient, "if it were not that pirate times are pretty well over, I should certainly say that craft sailed under the black flag!"

"Here! Mister L——," said the captain (suddenly addressing the reader's humble servant, the former narrator and present writer of this authentic narrative), "take the spy-glass, jump up aloft, and see what *you* can make out."

I did so; and, whilst ascending the rigging, may just as well make a fair start by explaining matters a little.

The above dialogue took place on the quarter-deck of the East Indiaman *Simoom*, Captain George Ponsonby, R.N., Commander, carrying, besides four mates, forty-five petty officers and foremast hands, together with a complement of twenty-five passengers, nearly all of whom were ladies either going out to join their husbands or find them; the East Indies then, as now, being a capital matrimonial market. We were a little over two months out from Gravesend, and the high land of the wild East coast of the Island of Madagascar was in sight, some ten or fifteen miles to leeward; whilst, midway between

THE STRANGE SAIL OFF MADAGASCAR.

our vessel and the shore, was the strange sail, standing off towards us, which had excited the suspicion of our senior officers.

I, the junior officer of that good ship—being no less a personage than the fourth mate—proceeded duly to establish myself in the mizen cross-trees, and keenly scrutinise the approaching stranger.

Mr. Mainstay had judged by the cut of her sails, for she was yet too distant for her hull to be seen from our decks. I, however, from my elevated perch, soon made out that her build was long, low, and rakish. She was schooner-rigged, and displayed an immense spread of canvas. Altogether, this craft presented the proverbial pirate appearances. Quickly descending to the quarter-deck, I made known the result of my observation. The captain told me to send his steward to him, and, when that functionary arrived, he ordered him to bring on deck his own telescope—an instrument never produced but on rare occasions, being a very powerful and valuable one, and, more than all, having been presented to him by the late Duke of Wellington, in recognition of services rendered that great general during the bombardment of the castle of Scylla in the time of the Peninsular war. Slinging this to his back, our commander, accompanied by his chief officer, climbed aloft to the position which I had lately vacated.

Of course, this proceeding—so unusual and portentous—attracted the attention of every one on board. All hands began clustering together in little groups, discussing the meaning of their superior's conduct, and glancing anxiously from the two figures in the mizen crosstrees to the suspicious sail under our lee. As for the crew, the younger sailors—scenting the battle afar off, and eager for a brush—betrayed visible symptoms of fierce delight, and seemed to like the prospect; but the older salts, shading their wrinkled eyes with their horny hands, and gazing in a quiet, discriminating manner at the cause of the excitement, ominously shook their heads. I heard one old fellow thus rebuke a youngster capering about in great glee at the prospect of a fight—

"Ay, ay, my hearty! shuffle away with your pins; you may be docked afore night. That 'ere craft carries a strong crew behind her bulwarks—or else call me a lubber! 'Taint a collier's starboard watch as could handle them 'flying kites' [1] and square-cut sails o' hern."

The passengers were in quite a flutter of excitement; the most terrifying rumours were being circulated from one to the other, without, it may readily be believed, decreasing in colouring during the process.

"Oh, Mister L——," cried a charming voice at my side, "do come into the saloon and see Lady Murray; she is so alarmed!"

[1] The light and lofty sails.

Instantaneously closing my spy-glass, and turning to salute the fair owner of that well-known voice, I left the watching of the strange sail to other eyes, and accompanied her below.

Lady Murray, surrounded by several other lady passengers, I found reclining upon the Transom sofas, having just revived from a fainting fit, into which the unguarded communication made by one of the gentlemen had thrown her. The delinquent, a rough and ruddy Irish colonel, proceeding to India to join his regiment in the old Company's service, was standing by, doing his best to remedy the mistake; but I did not think much of his tact, for I heard him exclaiming—

" Sure thin, my lady, don't be afraid! Every man Jack of us will be kilt ten times over before any blackguard spalpeen of a pirate shall harm you, that we will! Thin, you know, they don't make ladies ' walk the plank.' Ah, sure now, don't be after getting frightened, my deal madam! Why, me with my elephant-gun, and my trusty *sowar*, Ako, with his keen *tulwar*, are enough to protect you from a whole regiment—I mane, squadron—of pirates."

" Oh, Mister L——," cried Lady Murray, the moment she saw me enter the saloon, " pray tell us what is the matter! What is that horrible ship in sight? Colonel O'Brien alarmed me by coming to say that it was a pirate."

I strove to reassure her by truthfully enough declaring that the supposed evil character of the strange vessel was by no means certain; that, even supposing our suspicions were confirmed, we were quite capable of defending ourselves. Defend ourselves! Ay! for my part I felt determined enough to give any pirates a tough struggle who might venture to interfere with us and our lady passengers. That dear girl, her cheeks flushed, and her eyes sparkling with excitement, was watching me anxiously, and listening earnestly to all I said.

VIEW IN THE INTERIOR OF MADAGASCAR.

As I turned to leave the saloon, forgetting her caution, she laid her hand on my arm, exclaiming—

"Oh, Fred! tell me; is there any danger?"

"No, darling!" I replied in a whisper, as Lady Murray, having noticed the act of her beautiful young companion (such was the position she held), cried—

"Come, come, miss!—let Mr. L—— return to his duty. Why, I verily believe that you are becoming more frightened than myself! It was only the sudden shock given by this awful Colonel O'Brien's abrupt communication that overpowered me. I am not a bit afraid now, Lucy."

And the brave English gentlewoman stood up, her weak health, however, sadly belying her fearless expression, for she was deadly pale.

As for poor Lucy, she blushed violently, fearing her secret had been guessed at; then hid her confusion by embracing her friend and mistress with delightful tact.

At this moment the shrill piping of our boatswain and his mates rang echoing through the ship, followed by the hoarse command—

"All hands ahoy! All hands lay aft on the quarter-deck!"

Pressing the hand of the beautiful girl unseen, and bidding the ladies have no fear, I rushed up the companion-ladder and gained the deck, leaving the fire-eating colonel shouting to his orderly—

"Here, Ako, you rascal! Be quick and unpack my elephant-gun and rifles."

Ako placidly responded—"Ar-char, sahib!" (Very good, sir).

I found that the captain and chief officer had descended to the deck, and were awaiting the muster of the ship's company. As I made my appearance, I received an order to tell the steward to have some grog brought up ready to serve to all hands. This meant business. By the time that I returned to the side of my superior officers all hands had assembled. Without loss of time the captain proceeded to address them :—

"My lads," said he, "you all see that sail under our lee, and have no doubt remarked that, since she put out from the land at daylight, she has been bearing up for us, changing her course as we changed ours, and evidently. dodging us from the time she hove in sight. Well, many of you have, perhaps, heard of the famous Black Pirate,(') supposed to cruise in these latitudes ; in my opinion it is no other than that craft now trying to overhaul us. Now, my lads, I never believed in the existence of that marauder before ; I never heard any authentic intelligence bearing on the fact, often as I have sailed these seas, probably because the motto of the scoundrels chasing us is, 'Dead men tell no tales.' This alone will be enough to make us defend our vessel to the last, for no quarter can be expected from the pirates. They are, no doubt, a mixed scum of all nations, very likely largely composed of blacks from the land in sight. Now, men, will you let a horde like that capture our ship, or will you stand by me like true British seamen ?"

For a moment the perfect silence with which our crew had listened to their captain's speech reigned unbroken ; then the stalwart old boatswain rushed to the front, forgetting his rigid discipline, and cried—

"Come, my hearties, three cheers for Captain Ponsonby, and down with the pirates !"

Frantically waving his cap, whilst his silvered locks were tossing in the wind, the immediate controller of the crew led off a round

---

(') This was a famous pirate, some years ago, who became the terror of the Indian Ocean.

of such cheering as never came from the throats of any but English sailors. Then, pipe of silver in hand, and followed by his two mates, he moved to the side of his officers, awaiting orders.

A proud smile came athwart the bronzed features of our captain; a bright flash sparkled in his eyes. He glanced upon those strong and hardy seamen, so ready to execute his slightest will, then cast a look upon the strange sail under our lee, and I knew that he felt strongly moved to bear down and engage her.

"Thank you, my men! thank you!" he cried. "I knew that one and all would stand by me. No pirate shall hold these decks while two planks stick together and a man is left to tread them!"

Orders were now given to clear the decks and prepare for action, a work our tars proceeded to execute with alacrity.

"Mister Mainstay," said the captain, suddenly, "do you think that it would be possible to get at those government guns amongst the cargo?"

"Yes, I almost think so, sir," replied the chief officer, "but I will see what the second mate says."

The latter was sent for, and the captain continued—

"You see, it is very likely that craft may carry a 'Long Tom' amidships, and, if so, by keeping on and off, and playing at long bowls, she could easily knock us to pieces whilst herself keeping safely out of range of our carronades."

"That's a fact, sir," responded the mate. "And nearly all these small craft—letter of marque, pirate, or war vessel—carry one heavy pivot gun, to make up the weight of metal they are not large enough to carry on the broadside."

"Just so, Mister Mainstay; and if we could only get up one of those 'long thirty-twos' destined for the fort at Calcutta, it would be easy to rig it up amidships on the spindle of the after-deck capstan; then we should be a match for her."

The second officer now came up, and, in reply to the captain's inquiry, declared there would be no difficulty in getting one of the guns in question, which were all stowed under the main hatchway.

As soon as the decks were cleared, the guns cast loose, shot and shell handed up, the arm-racks filled, and everything made ready for action, the starboard watch was placed under the second mate's orders to break out the cargo and get up one of the guns in the hold.

From early morning, when the strange sail first hove in sight, we had been bowling along at the rate of seven knots an hour on a taut bowline; but, since the tropical sun had exerted its powerful rays, the wind had gradually fallen, so that now, shortly before noon, the speed of our vessel had become considerably reduced. This was soon made evident, for, though dead under our lee, she was rapidly diminishing the distance that separated us.

By the time that the "long thirty-two" had been hoisted up out of the hold, the hull of the pirate was plainly visible from our decks, and there no longer existed a doubt as to her character. By the aid of our glasses we could discern that not only was her hull of a uniform, unrelieved black, but that her spars and yards were also of the same sombre hue; these were the well-known characteristics described as pertaining to what every one on board had hitherto considered the mythical "Black Pirate." All hands were now becoming unpleasantly and optically convinced that the ambiguous reports were not so much without foundation as, perhaps, they had fondly imagined. Still, I do not believe that a man on board felt the slightest fear. It generally takes a good deal to frighten a sailor—especially a true British one— and our crew consisted entirely of Englishmen—a thing it would be impossible to find now-a-days, since the Indiamen of the old Honourable East India Company's service have become a tale of the past, and every merchantman carries a large proportion of foreigners on her articles.

Very fortunately, upon unshipping the after-deck capstan, we found that, by the help of a few wedges, the iron spindle would just fit into the carriage of the long gun, and so serve as its pivot—all the guns on freight being arranged upon the swivel principle, with frame and sliding-carriage to match, so that they each could sweep a complete circle. It was still more fortunate that out of our armament of ten carronades four were thirty-twos, the rest being eighteen pounders; thus we were not without proper fitting ammunition for our *impromptu* " Long Tom."

The suspicious-looking schooner was now within six or seven miles. We had just finished rigging the gun amidships, when she executed a manœuvre that would at once have dispersed any lingering doubt we might have entertained as to her intentions. Suddenly taking in all her square sails, she hauled right up in the wind's eye, laying a good three points nearer than we could, under a cloud of fore and aft canvas. No peaceful trader, and few men-of-war, ever spread such sails; for she carried immense stay-sails on every stay, besides taunt-rigged gaff-topsails above her huge mainsail and fore-and-aft foresail, with a large ringtail projecting beyond her mainsail, and a great jib-topsail bellying above her head-sails. Hitherto she had only been gradually closing with us through steering towards the same point as ourselves, her rig enabling her to lay a point or so nearer the wind than we could; whereas, a similar vessel to our own would have been running on a precisely parallel course, without getting any nearer. But now, with nothing but fore-and-aft sail set—and set, too, with the sheets hauled close aft, flat as boards—she bore up for us on a much more oblique angle, which threatened soon to bring the vessels close together.   Upon seeing this manœuvre, Captain Ponsonby held a consultation with his officers, at which I was present, and stated his views to the following effect :—

"Gentlemen," said he, "it is quite evident that if the wind lasts and does not increase, our pursuer will overhaul us some time before dusk, providing we hold our present course.   Now, I do not at all like the idea of running from an enemy ; but this is not a king's ship, and our first duty is to care for her safety, as well as for that of cargo and passengers.   Still, if you should think that anything is to be gained by meeting the pirate—who evidently means to attack us—I am quite prepared to bear down and engage her.   But if you agree with me, that our first duty is to try and avoid an encounter, then we will put the ship before the wind (her best sailing point).   We are fully forty miles from the land, and, this part of the coast being marked on the chart as free from dangers, we might run close in. We should thus stand a good chance of being able to evade our pursuer during the night, supposing the change of course enabled us to keep ahead."

We all agreed with our captain that "Defence, not Defiance" was our duty ; also, that it would be highly advisable to try the change of sailing he rightly recommended.   It is true, both I and the third mate were rather in favour of turning upon the pirate and attacking *him*, but we could not find fault with our experienced commander's sound judgment.

The course was altered.   The bowlines were let go ; the sheets and tacks eased off ; and the yards trimmed for running with the wind a point or two abaft the beam.   This enabled us to have not only the benefit of all fore-and-aft sail, but also studding-sails on the weather side. The effect was soon perceptible. The speed of our vessel visibly increased ; the straining, unpleasant motion of being close-hauled changed to the easy, rolling, and unchecked movement of running free before the wind. With snowy stun'-sails alow and aloft, projecting far beyond each weather yard-arm, with every stay·sail set that would draw, with sail crowded on even to the three lofty sky-sails and royal stun'-sails, for some time we seemed to hold our own in the race. But our wary pursuers, finding that by this means we should probably sail far beyond the line on which they had hoped to intercept us (because, instead of edging along it, we had changed our course, and ran direct to cross it), changed their tactics too, and put before the wind, though not to the extent we had, setting their square sails again, and doing their utmost to overhaul us. We knew that the change in our course would enable the pirate to gain the weather-gage, and get to windward of us, so as to hem us in between himself and the land ; but we did not care for this so long as it afforded the prospect of keeping clear of him till nightfall.

Alas! for our hopes. Still fell the wind, and every moment brought the enemy nearer and nearer. At length, flap went our outrigged stun'-sails, with that sullen sound so suggestive of approaching calm—at least, suggestive to the ear nautical. Our captain, who was standing by the quartermaster carefully conning the steering, gave a hasty glance aloft at the shaking canvas, then turned to his first officer and calmly said—

"Prepare for action, Mr. Mainstay, and have everything ready to shorten sail, to get those ' flying kites ' out of the way, as soon as the enemy get us within range."

The order was promptly executed. The guns were all loaded

with solid shot, the gunner, who had served in the same capacity in a king's ship with our captain, taking particular care with the loading of the "long thirty-two" we had rigged amidships, himself fitting a rope grummet over the shot, and ramming it home with extra force. The sailmaker and his mates placed in convenient places stoppers for splicing temporarily any important rope that might be shot away, whilst the carpenter's crew got ready plugs for stopping shot-holes, as well as spars for fishing any mast that might get seriously injured. Cutlasses and pistols were buckled on by the seamen, a select party of marksmen being armed with musket and bayonet and placed under the orders of Colonel O'Brien, who volunteered his services. The surgeon took up his quarters, and made his preparations for the wounded, in our ward-room, being, moreover, assisted by a clerical passenger, as also by Lady Murray and a strong-minded gentlewoman. The rest of the ladies were made as comfortable as possible in the after hold, where they were below the water-line, and safely out of range of the enemy's fire. All the remaining gentlemen, to the number of six, including the colonel, preferred to join in defence of the ship. As they were mostly military men, and had rifles of their own, they formed a valuable addition to the colonel's small marine force. The ropes of the running-gear, connected with the stun'-sails and other light canvas, were carefully coiled on deck in "Flemish coils," all ready for letting go, and so that no hitch might take place through a kink in a rope whilst shortening sail. The crew were then told off into two parts—one division to work the big guns; the other, to work the ship and act as small-arm men, as boarders, or however necessary. The party of marines belonged to this latter body, and those of them who were seamen were stationed in the mizen, main, and fore-tops, with a plentiful supply of ammunition.

The pirate was now almost within range, and he proved it by suddenly luffing up, firing upon us, and hoisting his colours. The gun fired was a "Long Tom," amidships, as our captain had expected. Any further doubts that might have been entertained by any one on board were now effectually set at rest, for, from the changed position of our pursuer, we saw the black flag run up at the same moment we were fired upon. The shot fell far astern, but it warned us that in a little while we should be under fire.

Being immediately under the captain's commands, I received his order to hoist our colours, and the red ensign of old England was soon fluttering from our peak. We did not think of replying to the pirate's shot, preferring to wait until our answer would be of some effect; but as that well-known flag shook its red folds above us, there burst from our crew so hearty and simultaneous a cheer as must have reached even to where the pirates followed nearly in our wake.

Flap, flap, went the canvas overhead, and the sails hung drooping from the yards. The concussion from that gun seemed to have stilled the last breath of air. For some little time both vessels lay perfectly becalmed. Not the gentlest zephyr came to ruffle the glassy smoothness of the sea; still the never-quiet waters moved heaving up and down in long and regular throbs, like the heavy respirations of some gigantic living thing, and every heave sent the useless canvas flapping heavily against the masts. Prudence would have told us to be glad at this, for evening was approaching, and if the calm lasted till dark it would prevent the pirate closing with us, whilst also giving us the chance to evade him by the aid of any breeze that might spring up during the night. But even this was not to be. Ere long we noticed a strange splashing of the water on either side of our enemy. Upon using our glasses, we discovered that this appearance was due to the pirate having put out long sweeps with which to propel himself forward. Here was a cause for alarm, as the scoundrels would be able to choose their own position, attack us how they pleased—even in directions upon which we could not bring a gun to bear—and, in fact, be able to manœuvre round and about us at discretion. It was a nasty fix to be in, and every one would not have known how to better the position ; but our captain was equal to the difficulty. Ordering a couple of boats to be lowered, he gave the chief officer instructions to prepare a drag by tossing a spare topmast overboard, towing it a good distance ahead of the ship, then fixing it by fastening to it a sail spread out and sunk by heavy weights suspended to its lower parts, the contrivance being made serviceable to swing the ship either way by bending on a couple of stout ropes to its centre, and bringing their other ends on board, one on the starboard, the other on the port quarter, where they would act as springs.

Within an hour the pirate had come so near that we could plainly see her decks were crowded with men. We could also hear the whooping and shouting of those encouraging themselves at the sweeps. The sun, setting unusually red in a crimson-tinted sky, was right in her wake, so that her black hull and spars seemed to us blacker still ; whilst even her sails, throwing their dark shadow between us and the sun, appeared of the same inky hue, and the long, projecting sweeps moved forward and backward like the ugly black legs of some monstrous multipede. As she came on thus, thrown out black, huge, and sinister against the blood-red background of the crimson sunset, she seemed to present a perfectly diabolical appearance, and this was made still more terrible when the fierce, fiend-like yelling of her pirate crew rang echoing through the surrounding silence of the still night air.

All day long the barometer had been rapidly falling, and the weather, though fine, had yet presented strange and unsettled symptoms, sufficiently ominous to the mariner who knew himself to be within the Mauritius hurricane zone, and that, too, just at the worst season. The storm was evidently brewing, and about to burst forth as the sun went down; the preceding temporary calm being an ordinary feature. The pirates seemed aware of this, and exerted all their energies to close with us before the tempest came to stay their plundering propensities.

On came that black, weird-looking schooner. We could now hear the creaking and jolting of the heavy sweeps as the pirate crew swayed to and fro at them with united strength and determination. Nearer and louder sounded their fierce yelling; and they seemed to be working themselves into a state of frenzy for the attack. They were now right under our stern, and steering straight for that part of our vessel; thinking, no doubt, to run us aboard in that defenceless position, when we would not be able to bring a gun to bear upon them. They were not aware of the means we had taken to meet this mode of attack. Closer and closer came our merciless assailants, till at length they were within fifty yards, when suddenly, ceasing to pull with their starboard sweeps, they brought their port broadside to bear, and poured into our stern a heavy raking fire. A perfect silence reigned fore and aft the decks of our vessel; but every man was at his post—every hand ready and willing to meet the foe! Our captain had seen the enemy's manœuvre, and met it by ordering his crew to throw themselves flat on deck; by which means they escaped the missiles of that first broadside, every shot passing harmless overhead or through the rigging, save two or three that crashed tearing into the woodwork of our stern, but did no further mischief than frighten the poor ladies down below.   The wild shouts and yells of the pirate crew formed a striking contrast to the steady silence of our own ; and, when they had lessened the distance between us by another thirty yards, this seemed to impress them; for their furious whooping subsided into a confused Babel of voices as they ceased pulling, sheered their vessel across our stern again, and poured in their starboard broadside.   They were now so close that, being themselves low in the water, nearly the whole of the grape and canister they this time saluted us with flew overhead, though the loud rattle made by such of the *mitraille* as lodged about the stern and quarters must have terribly alarmed the ladies again.   The discharge was not quite so harmless as the last, for two of our men were hit with grape-shot, one of them being badly, if not mortally, wounded.

The moment for which our captain waited had now arrived.

" Haul away, my lads !   Haul away with a will," he said to the men standing ready with that rope in their hands which had been led on board to the starboard quarter.

No second command was needed, for it was stamp and go with the men, and, as they stamped forward along the deck, firmly holding the rope, the ship was slowly swung round, and the port broadside brought to bear upon the astounded pirates.

Springing to the mizen rigging, our captain cried through his speaking trumpet—

" Are you ready, there, at the guns ?"

" All ready, sir," came promptly from each gunner, waiting match in hand.

" Then fire !" shouted the captain.

And a terrible broadside swept the decks of the pirate, as we knew by the cries and groans that instantly arose. Every gun had been double-shotted with an extra grape and canister charge on top of a solid shot, and, our ship standing high out of the water, we were consequently enabled to command and sweep the low decks of the pirate, lying open and exposed to our fire.

The sharp rattle of musketry mingled with the deafening roar of the cannonade, for our small-arm men poured in volley after volley, being loudly encouraged by their commander, the Irish colonel, who became very Hibernian when excited. The pirates were not yet daunted; and, while some of them kept up a heavy but ill-directed reply to our fusilade, others manned their sweeps again, and pulled forward to try and board us. This we were bound to prevent, for the schooner was full of men, whose overwhelming numbers would soon be able to vanquish us, if once they succeeded in gaining our decks.

Hauling away upon the port drag-rope, we brought our starboard-broadside to bear just as the pirate's prow was almost touching our bulwarks. The whole fore-part of the schooner was crowded with men ready to board.

The sun had now for some little time vanished below the western horizon, and the brief tropical twilight was already merging into the darkness of night, save for the deep red glow still radiating in the west. This ruddy sky being immediately behind the pirates, and there being so little daylight left, shed upon them a deeper, more blood-stained reflection than before. Now that she was close upon us, the whole fabric of the schooner stood out sharp and intensely black against the redly glimmering light behind. Her whole aspect was terrible and supernatural; the black figures of her crew clustering together in the bows, brandishing their arms, and leaping about, were more like fiends than men; their terrific yelling, in many a barbarous tongue, considerably strengthening the resemblance. The noise of the fray, the ceaseless sharp cracking of the musketry, the crashing roar of the cannon, the subdued groaning of the wounded and mangled, together with the yelling of the pirates and the hearty cheering of our own men, made a most hideous din—a frightful conflict of sound; whilst the incessant flashing of the small-arms, the great sheets of flame vomited forth by the cannon, and the fiery, sulphurous-smelling clouds of smoke occasionally enveloping both vessels, always twisting and wreathing about their rigging, gave the finishing accessories to the whole infernal scene.

On, then, came the pirate vessel, till her stem was close aboard us! But at that moment—when the savage wretches, clustering forward, were stringing their nerves to spring upon our decks—crash among them went the iron hail of our starboard broadside. The slaughter must have been frightful. Nothing could stand before the hurtling tempest of that terrible discharge, delivered with the muzzles of the guns almost touching the living objects in their front. For a moment or two the smoke obscured our view, but when it cleared away we saw that the lately crowded bows of the enemy were now empty, save where a dark and wide-spread heap lay still and prone upon the deck. But one form yet remained upright in the ghastly space our broadside had cleared, and the flash of a volley from our main-top showed me the blood-stained face. It was that of a huge, red-haired giant, so dressed that I knew him to be the captain of the pirates. He shook his fist menacingly towards us, then sprang from his exposed position, and, as he went aft, we could hear him ordering

REPULSE OF THE BLACK PIRATE.

his men in English to "back water" with their sweeps, so as to get away from us.

At this moment we were suddenly enlightened as to the state of the weather (which had been altogether neglected during the heat of the battle), by the bursting upon us of a sharp squall.

On looking around, we found that a heavy, arch-shaped, black cloud was just spreading above us, from which the huge rain-drops fell pattering slowly and loudly on the decks. We could hear the rushing, hissing noise of the wind tearing over the waters in the distance; but, before a rope could be started, right out from that sharply-defined cloud-arch the squall flew upon us. Crack, crack, went all our stun'-sail booms, each one snapping with a report like that of a gun. It was fortunate that the wind struck us from astern, sending us scudding before it, or more serious damage would have happened.

"Sky-sail, royal, and ta'-gallant halyards, let go!" roared our captain, as the gale came down; and, in obedience to his prompt commands, the ship was soon under easy sail.

Just then the pirates, having also shortened sail and made their vessel snug, ranged up and gave us a parting broadside. I felt a tremendous shock—a sharp and stunning blow—then fell senseless on the deck, my last thought being that a round-shot had taken off my head!

I knew not how long a time had elapsed, but, when I came to my senses again, I found myself suffering from a frightful headache; found, too, that I was lying, comfortably put to bed, in one of the vacant saloon state-rooms. I did not at first open my eyes, being almost afraid to do so, as I fully expected to find some important part of my body missing. At length, however, a long sigh, breathed close at hand, caused me to look up. Then the first thing that I saw, when my eyes opened again upon the world, was Lucy's fair face bending over me—love, grief, and anxiety all depicted on her beautiful features, and showing through the crystal tears that filled her streaming eyes. It was daylight, so I had been insensible a considerable time, and I could see Lady Murray sitting composedly reading in one corner of the little state-room. With a great effort I stretched forth one of my hands, grasped Lucy's white neck, and drew her lips to mine; for I knew not yet whether I should live or die, and, if the latter, determined to have at least one kiss before giving up the ghost—" kicking the bucket," I should have said, being a sailor. This proceeding brought back the colour to my darling's pale face, and, overjoyed at my recovery, she cried—

"Oh, Lady Murray, Fred is conscious again! *Will* he get well?"

"Why, of course, you foolish child!" said that lady, in so reassuring a tone of voice as to prove quite refreshing to *me*, and make me at once use my hands to feel how much there might be left of my former proportions.

"There is not anything the matter with him," continued that grateful voice of reassurance. "He has only received a—a—what did the doctor call it?—oh! a splinter wound and severe contusion. So do not alarm yourself, Lucy. He will be well in a day or two; and when we get to Calcutta I shall have the pleasure of accompanying you both to church the first fine morning before twelve o'clock."

This was doubly satisfactory to me. The course of our true love *was* to run smooth, I calmly reflected, despite the pain in my injured head; and she, who we had feared would prove an obstacle, was actually ready to arrange the match. I began to feel pretty well satisfied with the world in general—pirates included, for they had evidently brought about the *dénouement* that we were wont to dread. My head was still upon my shoulders: the girl I loved was being bestowed upon me *ex tempore* by the party holding authority to do so. I felt a hero. Like a hero, too, receiving the award of merit.

I began to think that I had in some way greatly distinguished myself during the engagement, though I could not remember how. The world, I reflected, whilst lying flat upon the broad of my Anglo-Saxon back, surveying things in a comfortable, dreamy, satisfied sort of way, was just beginning to appreciate my worth ; but, confound it! reflection increased the headache, so I gave it up, and merely squeezed Lucy's soft warm hand.

"Yes," continued Lady Murray, "now I know your secret, you sly puss ! I shall take care to see that you are both made happy, Your father gave you entirely into my charge, and I shall use my authority in a way that will please *you*, and, I have no doubt, satisfy *him*, for you might do worse. Mister L—— is a——"

But what flattering epithets were to be lavished upon me I know not, for Lucy, taking one of her burning hands from mine, placed it over the mouth of her kind-hearted mistress, who, I ascertained, had found out the state of our affections through the grief shown by her young companion when I had been carried below wounded. As for the injuries I had received, they were but trifling, and I often rejoiced in them, for had they not brought about the sanctioning of our attachment ?

I inquired after the " Black Pirate," but the ladies could only tell me that nothing had been seen of her after the engagement, and that it was believed she had gone down shortly afterwards. At all events, upon gazing shoreward through my cabin-port, not a sail or

THE LAST HEADLAND.

vestige of a vessel was in sight, and I only saw the last headland of Madagascar fast sinking out of view under our lee.

During several days I was confined to my cabin, and then felt loath to leave it, and so lose Lucy's tender nursing. However, whilst lying there, I may as well state how I became attached to that dear girl.

She did not come on board as a stranger, for I had, singularly enough, seen her twice before. On the first occasion, she had attracted my attention one night at the opera, when I could do nothing but gaze on her exquisite beauty, totally oblivious of the claims upon my attention, which should have been bestowed on the unfortunate sisters in my party. In fact, my gentle-tempered youngest sister, as we were leaving, was driven to ask in a spiteful manner,

"When do you go to sea again, Fred?" And she said it, too, as though mentally exclaiming, "I trust it may be soon!"

Upon encountering Lucy a second time, I was more fortunate. Two or three days before the *Simoom* was ready for sea I determined to run down to Woodford, and say good-bye to an uncle living there. My relative was a crusty old fellow, and the leave-taking did not occupy much time. I had just reached the high road, when, upon coming within sight of the old "Green Man," I saw the four-horse, scarlet-painted mail-coach drive up to the door amidst a cloud of dust. A female figure alighted therefrom, and came walking towards me on the High Beach road. At first, in the distance, I could not tell whether she were young or old, plain or pretty; nevertheless, a strange sensation seemed to thrill my nerves even at the very moment when first my eyes rested upon her. Perhaps believers in animal magnetism can explain it, I cannot. I wonder whether the electro-biologists can?

Nearer she came, yet nearer. An unaccountable hesitation seemed to possess me. I felt a strange attraction to that advancing form. My first distinct impression was of a bright ray of sunshine reflected from a glittering golden curl. She had now approached so near, that I could discern her features. I recognised them instantly, and felt as I had never done but once before—as I had never felt in the presence of any woman but herself. That mysterious spell, the power of beauty and an innate sympathy, held me with its resistless fetters.

We men have nearly all, I suppose, at some period of our lives, pictured to ourselves our ideal Venus: well, mine was before me. There glided the fairy form hitherto worshipped in my nightly visions and daily dreams. No longer an impalpable shadow, but a veritable

mortal of flesh and blood, filled with the same warm life and sen-
sibility as myself—a being one could love, adore, and, more than all,
be loved by in return!   Oh, how my heart yearned towards thee,
my lovely Lucy, even as we saw each other for the second time
in our lives!

As the fair girl whose beauty had so powerfully attracted me at
the opera now passed me on the road, she noticed my earnest gaze,
and started, as she probably recognised the rude fellow whose per-
tinacious staring had disconcerted her on the former occasion. Averting
her head, she walked quickly away, as though I frightened and might
insult her. Good heavens! I could not have found sufficient boldness
to accost her even had it been to save my life.   I, the reckless young
sailor, usually so well at my ease with the fair sex, stood abashed and
speechless.   Timid and hesitating, I remained watching her receding
figure, undecided whether to turn and follow, or pass on and lose her,
perhaps for ever.   Furtively I glanced around, fearful lest the prying
eye of some curious stranger might detect me, an inquisition from
which I shrank with extreme aversion.   My apprehensions were,
however, quite groundless.   Not a soul was in sight to mark or
ridicule my conduct.   That beauteous form was fast receding in
the distance.   I could never have found courage enough to turn and
follow, but the mystic cord that bound me to her began to tug at my
heart-strings, and, mechanically as it were, I commenced retracing
my steps.   As I walked along, she once turned her head and saw
me, then, I fancied, quickened her pace in order to avoid me. Shortly
afterwards, round a bend in the road, we came upon a neat little
cottage nestling amidst the foliage of a flourishing garden ; an instinc-
tive perception told me that it was the destination of her I followed.
Sure enough, she raised the latch of the garden-gate and vanished

within the flower-covered portico. My heart beat with gratification. I had, at all events, ascertained either the residence of her to whom fate had attracted me, or that of some of her friends.

The surrounding country was uncultivated forest land, and all the rest of that afternoon, from my hiding-place among the brambles, the waving heather, and the sweet-smelling wild flowers, I kept strict watch upon the door of the cottage. I knew that I had missed the coach to London, but what cared I, so long as it gave me the chance of meeting that beautiful girl again? It became dusk, and I was obliged to find a nearer spot from whence to continue my vigil. The road was very lonely. I began to think that perhaps robbers might attack the cottage during the night. I did not, at the time, perceive the absurdity of the idea—fixing upon *that* night, when thieves had never yet thought it worth their while to molest the retired abode, long as it had stood. Still, as the hours sped and it grew darker, I began to fancy every shadow a stealthy burglar. How I hoped that such might prove the case, in order to give me the opportunity of introducing myself, and the satisfaction of saving *her* from danger! I could no longer rest in the place I had chosen. Starting up, I moved towards the cottage, noticing as I did so that lights were gleaming through the half-closed shutters of a room on the ground-floor. In a moment I was gliding to the spot. Had any burglars been about, they would certainly have claimed me for one of their choice fraternity, as with cautious step I stole silently towards the windows. Upon getting within the shadow of the walls, I crept up to the nearest panes, and eagerly peered through.

How delightful were my sensations during the next few moments! I gazed at the beautiful maiden with an absorbing interest. Unseen, alone, perfectly at my ease, I studied her every movement with the

P

keen, fresh pleasure one feels in scanning for the first time some glorious work of nature.

Four persons were seated around the parlour-table. One of them—at a glance I saw he was the father of my charmer—was reading prayers to the others. Lucy's mother sat by his side, whilst she herself was immediately facing me. A servant made up the party. For the first time during many months, if not years, I really felt in a proper state of mind to pray : I longed to join that simple, honest, happy circle. Prayers being ended, I had the satisfaction to hear the old man say to his daughter—

"Fetch me the paint and brush, my darling; the coach starts at eight in the morning, so I had better finish addressing your luggage to-night."

So she was to return to town in the morning : by the same conveyance, too ! The work of addressing her trunks made me gaze on with redoubled interest. An extraordinary coincidence was about to happen—a far stranger event than the fact of my meeting that fair girl a second time by accident. The last box was nearest to the window, and, to my intense amazement, I plainly saw the old man paint the name of my ship.

Yes, there it was, as plain as large white letters could make it— *Simoom !*

The rest I could not make out, but imagination supplied the missing link ; those smaller letters could never be anything else than " Passenger per."

Just then the servant came to fasten up the windows, and I was forced to beat a rapid retreat. All night long, heated with excitement and worrying myself with innumerable conjectures, from my leafy covert I lay watching the cottage, and only dozed off for a few minutes before daylight; but then I indulged in innumerable cheroots. And when that sun arose, how bright, how beautiful, how happy all creation seemed in its resplendent rays! Ah, it was indeed a happy day for me—the commencement of my new life. I thought of fifty different ways to introduce myself to her I so patiently awaited; but my boldness had vanished, utterly vanished, and I could not make up my mind how in the world to act. Of one thing, however, I was determined—not to miss her; no matter where she might go, I would follow, and make her acquaintance.

It is needless to describe how impatiently I awaited the coming forth of my fair one. However, time is fleeting, as all the world knows to its sorrow; and though it may seem long to wait for a thing we ardently desire, when it has come and passed, then how short we think its duration! So Lucy at length appeared with her father, and, while a light cart took forward her luggage, she walked with him in the direction of the "Green Man"—the coach post-house. I saw that her eyes were tearful, and knew that she had had a sorrowful parting with her mother; but then it did not make *me* sorry: rather the reverse, for it encouraged the belief that she must be bound on a long journey, and I thought of the *Simoom* painted on her boxes. Was she really one of our passengers?

Not wishing to be seen in my unwashed state, I made a *détour* to avoid them, and ran for the hotel, getting there long before they did, making myself tidy, and snatching a rather hasty breakfast before the coach was ready to start. I found that we were the only passengers from Woodford, yet I bit my lips upon feeling too bashful to go inside with her, and then sullenly took an outside place. Several times, just before the coach was ready to start, I had been quite near her, and fancied that her look, when she recognised me

again, partook as much of satisfaction as surprise. Vanity is natural
to every human being, from the South Sea Islander who takes delight
in a huge fishbone-ring through the nose, or the Chinese beauty who
cripples her feet, to the London belle who deforms her waist—and
all like to be admired. Admiration was plainly expressed in my
gaze. I could notice that every now and then she gave sly little
glances at me, taking care, as she thought, that neither I nor her
father should observe them. After all, I was not such a bad-looking
fellow in my fourth mate's uniform ; but she *may* have had an idea
that I had been to Woodford upon the same errand as herself—to
bid my friends good-bye—and such being the case, her curiosity may
have been aroused as to whether I belonged to the *Simoom*.

After a painful parting with her father, she entered the coach,
and we were off. From my place on the front seat I was much
gratified to find that I could fairly survey, through a convenient little
ventilator, the sweet features of the solitary inside passenger.

She was very, very beautiful. The heavy masses of her pure
golden hair waved and twined in rich and wonderful profusion
around her small, straight brow. So luxuriant were these glorious
tresses, that there seemed a difficulty in confining them within reason-
able limits, as was denoted by the massive natural braids drawn so
closely and tightly together—oh, ye unfortunate damsels whom cruel
fate has driven to take refuge in the help of *chignon !* Crisp little
curls of a golden fringe clustered along her forehead and over the
delicate little ears, and the same rippling wave extended the whole
length of her beautiful hair. Who can describe the glorious colour
of those splendid tresses ? Her head seemed bound with a coronet
of living, serpentine gold, and this gave that faint golden tinge which
makes the pink and white complexion of such fair-haired women so

exquisite. Deepest blue, violet, grey, those large, almond-shaped eyes took sometimes one hue, sometimes the other. Those mirrors of the soul, how I delight to gaze into their bright, living, mystifying depths! The pupils of those magical orbs were large—unusually large—and dilated with the least excitement; such eyes talk, they do not look. The lashes were long and drooping, and it was strange what expressiveness dwelt in the almost black eyebrows, that were ever moving, ever varying, ever telling of the emotions. Features so regular, so purely Grecian, I had never before seen. Her face was a perfect oval, and the small, straight nose was of the most delicate and sensitive chiseling. Those lips beneath! those warm, ruby, luscious lips, contracting or unfolding with every phase of feeling, and both so exquisitely carved, so small—yet full and large enough—so sweet, and only parting to show such tiny pearly teeth, set in such pretty pink coral! It was really sinful to think that mouth was made for aught but angels' kisses!

* * * * * *

"There! For gracious sake turn away your head, Lucy, and do not sit watching me as I write; it will make 'my own yarn' a rhapsody, instead of the true and faithful narration of how we met, and how the adventure with the 'Black Pirate' brought about the settlement of our attachment," I have just been forced to exclaim, pushing back my papers as that fair face came provokingly near, and the little figure bent over me in all its undulating gracefulness.

* * * * * *

Well, to resume the thread of my story, and get back to where we left off in the cabin of the *Fortuna*.

* * * * * *

I was congratulating myself on the capital position I had

obtained, and wondering how to find an opportunity of addressing her whom I was watching, when, with a sudden crash, over went the coach, and I found myself flying through the air like a sky-rocket—only, however, to come down like the stick. My next impression was of a rather prickly nature, as, luckily for my bones, if unfortunately for my flesh, I found myself uncomfortably seated in the centre of a huge furze-bush growing by the roadside. Directly I escaped from the thorns I ran to the door of the coach, and, after extracting a stout old female whom we had only taken up a moment or two before the accident, saw Lucy lying, apparently insensible, on the lower side of the capsised vehicle. Directly that bunchy old party was out of the way, I crept inside the coach, and raised *her* prostrate form in my arms. As consciousness returned to her, our eyes met, and were then averted in mutual embarrassment; but I fancied that a ray of pleasure stole into her glance, and that she did not look upon my assistance as the ordinary help of a stranger. The half-averted face turned full upon me, the softness of the drooping orbs became changed, and she exclaimed—

"What has happened ? Let me go, sir. Do not hold me so tight."

I felt loath to part with that slender yet beautifully-developed form, but, the horses beginning to kick and plunge, I at once helped her out of the coach. The cause of the break-down was explained by one of the fore-wheels lying in the road. We found the conductor attending to his insensible driver, and perfectly oblivious to the torrent of abuse being lavished on him by the disconsolate old party we had first extricated, and who was bitterly lamenting the untimely fate of a large basket-full of eggs.

As evidently nothing could be done without assistance to repair or right the vehicle, after helping to release the horses I offered my arm to Lucy, and we walked forward towards Leytonstone, where the required assistance would be found. We left the conductor to look after coach and driver, whilst that vociferous British female remained to bully him. It was the last we saw of her; for all I know to the contrary, she may yet be there, bewailing the loss of her eggs.

From Leytonstone we went on to London by another coach, and, before ending the journey, had become capital friends. The fact that she was one of the *Simoom's* destined passengers, and I one of that good ship's officers, afforded us ample material for wonder, satisfaction, and conversation. I left her at the door of Lady Murray's residence. She came on board with the rest of the passengers at Gravesend. Long before arriving within sight of Madagascar and the " Black Pirate," we had confessed our love—confessed it often, whilst hand in hand together, lulled by the pleasing murmur of the rippling waters, and subdued by the glorious splendour of the starlit tropical skies. But it was the pirate adventure that sealed our engagement, by discovering it to her who, we had feared, would not approve our plans.

As for the " Black Pirate," we never saw her more, neither did any one else, for she was never heard of again. After I had been carried below, the engagement was continued by our captain chasing the pirate, pouring in broadside after broadside of double-shotted guns to try and sink her, until the increasing gale compelled him to attend only to the safety of his own ship. But several of our best-sighted tars afterwards solemnly avowed that they had seen her go down head-foremost in the distance, not ten minutes after we fired our last gun. Considering that no rumours were ever again rife as to the existence of that once much-dreaded buccaneer, there seems no reason to doubt the truth of their statement; especially as our gunner affirmed, in an equally positive manner, that he had given her no less than fourteen shots between wind and water (all from the formidable " Long Tom " our captain's foresight had made us rig up amidships), and as the heavy gale that separated us must have severely tested her, if so badly injured.

Lady Murray kept her promise.　She did accompany Lucy and myself to church, before twelve o'clock, and on the first fine day after our arrival at Calcutta.　We returned to England, and I gave up the sea, for it had given me a treasure I valued far too much to ever risk losing by trusting to its changeful and uncertain moods, though I have ventured to return to the East this once; but it shall be the last time, for all the property in the world shall never induce me to leave my darling Lucy again.

THE LOG.

Seven Bells, 11*h.* 30*m. p.m.*—My friends greeted the conclusion of "my own yarn" with a perfect tempest of applause, and, as we drew up our chairs to the heavily-laden supper-table, extorted from me such further and minute particulars concerning the fair Lucy as I prefer leaving to the kindly imagination of my readers.

"Keep it up, thin! Keep it up, me boys!" shouted the doctor, directly after supper. "Sure thin, where's the use of going to bed—'turning in,' I mane?"—(he caught old Jack's indignant look, and corrected the unnautical expression.) "Let us keep it up till daylight! Put it to the vote!"

"Hear, hear!" roared Jack Backstay.

"Now thin, me boys, all you who vote for keeping it up till morning just hold out your right hands." Up went every right arm in the assembly. "Hooroo! Carried *nem. con.*," cried the doctor, his eyes glistening with satisfaction, and his hair, like "quills upon the fretful porcupine," all standing up in his excitement.

After the feast of reason and the flow of wit had lasted several hours, in conjunction with the flow of generous punch, beyond the grosser feast of supper, Mr. Lawrence proposed that we should finish up with another yarn. This occasioned some dispute as to who should be the narrator, the point being eventually settled by drawing lots for it, or, rather, "tossing," odd man out. Esmond was left in, and so to him fell the lot of spinning the last yarn—of ending, as well as commencing, our story-telling arrangement. Forthwith he gave us the following account of one of his seafaring experiences.

CAPTAIN DOBSON'S REVENGE.

AN ADVENTURE IN THE SEA OF AZOF.

THAT good brig the *Mary Jane*, of Sunderland—of which vessel I had the honour to be second mate—having duly delivered her cargo of coals at the Austrian port, Trieste, departed thence in ballast, and shaped her course for Taganrog, a Russian port on the Sea of Azof. This same Taganrog is a pretty large town, and a famous grain port. The worst of it is, however, that during at least two-thirds of the year it is frozen up, so that such vessels as arrive there late in the season, run a great risk of becoming ice-bound during the whole of the long and dreary winter.

The *Mary Jane* did not grapple to Azof mud until the 3rd or 4th of October, and at the end of that month the ice generally begins to set in. We lay, with other vessels, at a distance of twenty miles from the shore. In fact, Taganrog itself was not in sight, and we only knew of our position by seeing all along the coast, far as the eye could reach, the various craft moored here and there about the extended anchorage. The position of the port was indicated by the lighthouse on a nasty reef of rocks, and by a range of high hills in its immediate vicinity, though, as a rule, the great extent of shallow water terminated at an almost level beach of low, muddy, marshy land.

Our captain was a tall, hot-tempered,. sanguine-complexioned North-countryman, and being naturally anxious to escape a freezing delay of nine months, made many raids upon the peace and quiet of the slow-going, even-tempered agent he had selected—for he owned the *Mary Jane* himself.

M. Petroplopsky, the gentleman referred to, lived in a large house, in a street with a perfectly unpronounceable, even unspellable name, which formed the seaward view of Taganrog.

Large flat lighters are used to load the shipping at the distant anchorage, and half-a-dozen of them had brought us off half our cargo, when bad weather came on, and for one whole day no signs of a lighter could be seen. This made the captain mightily wroth, and at daylight on the following morn he came into my berth, roused me from my sleep, and roared rather than said—

"Come, turn out, Mister! Get the long-boat rigged, and ready for a trip to the shore. Not a lighter is in sight. That infernal son of a sea-cook of an agent means to have us frozen in here—he does, sir—by Jehoshaphat, he does!"

Captain Dobson was a Primitive Methodist and a religious man, and never used bad language—wonder of wonders for a seafaring member of society! Only when exceeding wroth or highly excited did he even use such inoffensive and strange expletives as the above. He never swore, and never allowed others to do so in his presence. At first he would seriously remonstrate with them; then, if that did not do, quietly knock them down. I thought his plan original, to say the least; pretty successful, too, for blasphemous oaths and foul language seldom sounded abaft the foremast, nor before it either, when some weather-beaten old tar would say to his shipmates, "Look out, my hearties, here's the 'old man' coming for'ard!"

In response to my commander's hail, I quickly sprang from my narrow little bunk, was dressed in a few moments, and then set to work at executing his orders.

In a vessel such as the *Mary Jane* there are seldom more cats than can catch mice ; so only a boy could be spared to join me in composing the long-boat's crew.

The hands looked rather doubtful and surprised when I turned them out to get the boat alongside, make ready her sails, fill up her water-beakers, and stow a small supply of provisions in the stern sheets, for the weather had a very lowering and threatening appearance.

Away seaward a thick, bluish grey haze covered the horizon, and rested with a sickly tinge upon the water. Nearer overhead huge masses of inky-black cloud flew swift and fierce towards the land, over which they formed a dense, black barrier, through which the suppressed light of the rising sun shone with a weird, red, and lurid glare. The waters were of the same dark, leaden hue as such patches of sky as now and then might be detected between openings of the sombre clouds, and black, smoke-like wreaths of flying scud. The sea splashed against our bows, and rippled all around with a dull, melancholy, metallic sort of sound; whilst strange murmurs—strange whining and sobbing noises—echoed through the air. Everything betokened the near approach of elemental strife.

However, I knew that nothing could shake the "old man's" determination when once he had made up his mind. So I did not say anything, but quietly put a couple of life-buoys in the boat.

After snatching a hurried breakfast, the captain, myself, and the boy entered the boat, made sail, and set off for the shore.

During the last two or three days it had been blowing a pretty

THE LIGHTHOUSE OFF TAGANROG.

heavy gale, but since the last sunset the wind had greatly moderated, and the sea had gone down. So, in spite of the threatening appearances, we made rapid progress before a stiff, fair breeze. As we passed the lighthouse at a distance of less than a quarter of a mile, it was with no little astonishment that we beheld a female form upon the balcony at its summit, gazing out upon the storm, with her long hair streaming on the blast. However, the old grey lighthouse and its strange tenant were soon out of sight astern. In less than four hours we were safe alongside the quay, and Captain Dobson rushed fiercely off towards the unhappy agent's house. Scarcely, however, had he stepped ashore, when down came the full fury of the gale, and for several hours the storm-fiend did his worst, revelling in the lightning and thunder, the furious blast, and the angry sea.

After a time the "old man" came down to the jetty, accompanied by the agent, who made a queer figure, muffled up in furs, and so bothered by the fierce gusts of wind as to be quite unable to do anything, save take care of himself and hold on to his clothes.

As it was quite impossible to attempt beating off for twenty miles against the gale, and with a small open boat, the captain tried hard to induce some Russian boatmen, who owned many large-decked fishing craft, lying moored along the jetties, to take us on board. But although he offered twenty-five pounds to any who would undertake the trip, not one dared venture.

Towards evening the gale began to moderate, and the aspect of the heavens was such as to indicate that it would soon subside into a snow-storm.

In spite of the agent's urgent entreaties that he would not venture out in the gale, Captain Dobson took his place in the long-boat, and commanded me to shove off from the quay and make sail.

He had transacted his business with the agent, and was naturally anxious to get back in charge of his ship before worse weather might place her in danger.

The Russian boatmen jabbered together most vociferously, and shrugged up their shoulders at our, to them, foolhardy conduct; whilst the agent stood wringing his hands, and calling upon the captain to return.   But he settled himself down to the tiller, bowsed aft the main-sheet, and away we sped on the first tack, dashing and plunging through the angry seas with bumps that threatened to start every plank, but, nevertheless, making very fair headway under our reefed cutter sail.

It was bitterly cold; the salt spray kept dashing and beating upon us heavily, and it was terribly hard work beating up and handling the heavy long-boat against both wind and sea.

As the darkness crept on, it grew yet colder, whilst the wind gradually fell, and, by the time we had made half the distance to the brave old *Mary Jane*, the snow came on, and we could no longer find our way, for the different vessels became hidden in the whirling, eddying, thickly-packed, pure white flakes that fell so densely, so gently, and with such inexhaustible determination.   As it was now impossible to find our vessel, all that we could hope to do was to see some other craft, on board of which we might obtain shelter for the night, or until the snow-storm had sufficiently abated to permit our proceeding in quest of the *Mary Jane*.

Blinded by the driving spray and the thickly-falling snow-flakes, for nearly an hour we drove wildly on at the mercy of the winds and water, when suddenly the boy, whom I had placed on the lee-side to keep a look-out, cried—

"There's a vessel to loo'ard, sir.   Here, we're close aboard her."

" Slack away the halyards," roared the captain, as he pushed the tiller over, and luffed up head to wind.

I did so, and, as the sail came down, saw that we were close aboard a small vessel, of which, in another two minutes, had we held our course, we should have been right athwart hawse, when in all probability the boat would have been capsized either upon her cable or under her bows, and we should all have found a damp grave at the bottom of the Azof Sea.

By lowering sail, and luffing head to wind, the boat quickly lost headway, so that we did not run out of sight of the vessel, and wind and sea gradually drifted us down alongside of her, as we put out a couple of oars to alter our position as necessary.

Before getting alongside the *xebec*, Captain Dobson hailed her several times in tones sufficiently stentorian to have awakened Rip Van Winkle, and at length managed to elicit a reply from the drowsy fellow on anchor-watch; but his words were of some strange, unknown tongue, so that we were unable to tell whether he gave us permission to come alongside or bade us keep off.

In spite of our lost and uncomfortable position, I felt a strange and unaccountable aversion to take shelter on board the foreigner. Besides, the unknown language and the look-out man's reply had sounded harsh and disagreeable. The vessel's hull and spars loomed black, dim, and sinister through the white and thickly-laden atmosphere around. Perhaps these things affected me. A rope was thrown to us, we got on board the stranger, and, carrying up the end of the painter, passed our boat astern.

By the dim light of a lantern held close to our faces, we were enabled to scan the very ill-favoured features of the look-out man and his captain ; the latter having, I suppose, been called on deck to

Q

receive us.   They were swarthy, black-muzzled, villanous-looking fellows, especially the captain, who scowled at us beneath his beetle brows, and made not the slightest attempt to treat us with the hospitality which had long been honoured as an indispensable custom at Taganrog : all vessels treating kindly the crews of such boats as, from the extent of the anchorage, and distance to the shore, frequently became belated either by night or bad weather.

By using what few words I chanced to know of that strange jargon, the "lingua Franca" of the Mediterranean, I ascertained that our inhospitable interlocutors were Greeks.   So much for the modern representatives of glorious and classic ground!

We were marched aft, then the Greek captain pointed out to us the round-house over his vessel's wheel (an edifice in which Greek and Italian craft do largely rejoice).   From the gesticulation to which we were treated, we derived the information that we could sleep there. We entered, and were left in total darkness, for the ill-natured and un-sailor-like lubbers would not even leave their miserable lantern with us ; but by-and-by I found out their reason for not doing so. Stumbling over small sails, coils of rope, swabs, brooms, buckets, and such-like varied ship's paraphernalia, we seated ourselves in the dark, and munched the beef and biscuit, and drank the cold water that we had brought up out of the boat.

Never before had I taken refuge on board a vessel in Taganrog roads, without having hot coffee and supper prepared for my party. Greeks, however, bear an evil reputation among sea-faring folk, and so we did not much wonder at our reception, neither did we growl ; but, directly the comfortless meal had been dispatched, spread ourselves out as well as we were able, and sought relief in slumber. Within half an hour the loud, healthy, trumpet-like snoring of my captain, and the soft, regular respiration of the boy, told me that my companions were fast and sound asleep.

As for myself, I could not close my eyes. Of a naturally restless disposition, my wakefulness was this night increased by the indefinable suspicion or presentiment with which I had become possessed. Moreover, I had noticed the keen glances darted by the Greek captain at the large "ditty-bag" (a canvas bag in which a sailor keeps his own tools, marling-spike, serving-mallet, sail-making implements, &c.), carried by our rough, unpretending, old-fashioned captain, in place of a more pretentious carpet-bag or valise. I knew that, on this occasion, among other things, the "ditty-bag" contained a pretty large sum of money, the skipper having obtained sufficient from the agent to find all hands in funds for a couple of days' liberty ashore. I could not help wondering whether the Greek divined its contents. He must have noticed that it seemed heavy, and that our "old man" took particular care of it ; besides, it was a common thing for captains to be returning on board their vessels with money from the shore. Then, again, I well knew the particularly unscrupulous nature of these modern Grecian mariners, many of whom either are, have been, or intend to be, pirates about the Archipelago. This knowledge, combined with my suspicions, and the gloomy effect of natural causes, gave me a preternatural sort of information and intelligence, which told my excited senses plainly enough that we were to be robbed, if not murdered. I kept my fears to myself, not only because they *might* prove groundless, in which case I did not care to endure the ridicule of my shipmates, but because I knew that our sole chance to escape with life, if attacked, was by quietly submitting ; whereas, if Captain Dobson came to suspect such treatment, his impetuous temper would be sure to burst forth. though, if suddenly set upon, he would most likely either be too surprised to resist, or else be over-powered at once, before he could inflict any serious damage upon the robbers, and drive them to extremities.

I know not how long a time had elapsed during these gloomy forebodings, for they did not keep the bell going on board the Greek, when, on a sudden, I became aware that the door of the round-house was being opened. Softly and stealthily it moved, and, as the opening became larger and larger, I perceived that the weather had cleared, for the moonlight plainly showed me the dark shadows of several men.

Slowly, inch by inch, the frail wooden thing that separated us from these midnight robbers was removed, though every now and then a stoppage occurred, as I saw the shadow nearest the door bend down in a listening attitude. No doubt convinced by our snoring and heavy breathing (for I now shammed sleep myself), the man at the door swung it quite open. Just then a ray of moonlight glittered like a streak of fire upon something in his hand.

Softly and silently I put one arm behind me, and felt for a weapon with which to defend myself. But nothing could I find ; my hand came in contact with nothing but coils of rope. And now my heart was beating and palpitating with great heaves and throbs that could be heard, for the intruder was crawling towards *me*, knife in hand, and I dared not obey the promptings of fear by springing up to combat him or escape. No, I had to endure the terrible suspense of remaining perfectly still and quiet, shamming sleep, when I knew not whether the next instant would find his knife in my heart or merely his hand in my pocket. Fortunately, I had self-possession enough both to know that the latter was by far his most likely intention, and to remain perfectly quiet whilst waiting for the proof; but it was terrible work, and I felt the great beads of perspiration rolling down my forehead, cold as I had been but a few moments before, whilst every nerve thrilled with a keen and exquisite sense of mental agony. Never, as long as I live, can be forgotten the feelings that I experienced during that long, long moment!

With a powerful effort I managed to restrain the almost irrepressible shudder that began to creep over my flesh as I felt the hands of the secret enemy upon me.

I knew now why

THE GREEK CAPTAIN.

the wretches had refused to leave a lantern with us—they feared that it might keep us awake.

By the faint light of the moon I had seen the dark form of the Greek captain bending over me, holding a long and formidable poniard between his teeth, whilst, with the adroitness of a practised thief, he softly, almost imperceptibly, and rapidly ran his hands over my clothes and pockets.

The pale light in the place contrasted with the lurid glare of the Greek's fierce black eyes. It was a dark, swarthy, ill-favoured face, and its cruel, ruthless expression told how little compunction its possessor would have had in cutting our throats.

The tremor of my limbs, as I violently repressed the inclination to shudder, perhaps startled him; for with one hand he suddenly snatched his dagger, and held the point within an inch of my throat, whilst with the other abstracting all the wealth about me—a sum of five roubles.(¹)

Then the infernal scoundrel passed on to the boy, found nothing there, and crept upon our captain.

The head of the "old man" had slipped off his pillow—the "ditty-bag," into which the plunderer's hands were quickly thrust. He was there but one moment, then stepped quickly back, sprang lightly over me, and was out of the round-house, the metallic chink as he went telling that he had obtained the money.

I waited some time, perhaps an hour, then went on deck. It was a fine night now. The moon was high and bright in the heavens, and a leading wind between our vessel and the shore was blowing fresh and steady. I went forward to the Greek on anchor-watch, got him to help me, and hauled the long-boat alongside. Then I went back to the round-house, awakened the boy and captain, told the latter of the change in the weather, and hurried him into the boat without giving him time to search his bag, which was carefully deposited in the stern-sheets, minus the cash for which all the care was taken.

(¹) A Russian coin worth about three shillings and sixpence.

I waited until the Greek *xebec* was out of sight, and we were within half a mile of the good old *Mary Jane*, before telling the captain of his loss. At first he was furious, and repeatedly called upon the name of Jehoshaphat in vain; but he soon agreed that by keeping quiet I had saved our lives, though he called upon the above-mentioned ancient Bible king to witness an oath that he would recover the money from the Grecian robber.

It was about two o'clock in the morning when we crossed our vessel's gangway.

"Call all hands, sir!" cried Captain Dobson, the moment we touched her decks.

The men, astonished at so unexpected a summons, came running aft in every style of *déshabille*.

In few and forcible words their commander told them of his loss, and called upon them to support him in taking the law into his own hands, and recovering the money.

A loud and hearty British cheer was the response. Arms were brought on deck, the *Mary Jane* was left in charge of the boy and the cook; then all the rest of us, nine in number, went into the long-boat, and off we went in search of our noble Grecian.

After an hour's sail we came to the spot where I expected to find her, for I had taken particular notice of her position, and had observed the bearings of several vessels in the distance, but she was not to be seen. Captain Dobson was furious at the thought that the pirates had fled, and gone clear off with his money. After cruising about for nearly an hour in vain, I happened to look up at the massive old lighthouse from which the gleaming golden rays came streaming through the darkness of the early morning; the sight of it at once inspired me with a sudden thought.

"Captain," I said, "do you think the lighthouse people may have seen the *xebec* get under-weigh? Perhaps she has only shifted her anchorage, for fear we might return to identify her."

" Bravo! That's right, my boy," replied the skipper. " Let us try, anyhow.

It was with some difficulty that we managed to effect a landing upon the rock on which the lighthouse stood; this accomplished, we at last succeeded in making the inmates hear us. A door about twelve feet above us was opened, and, a slight wooden ladder being passed down, we were enabled to enter the building and make inquiries.

The female, whom we had seen revelling in absorbed contemplation of the storm and tempest, proved to be the only daughter and companion of the old Greek mariner installed as keeper of the lighthouse. She was a handsome young woman, with pale, classic features, long raven hair, and deep-black, dreamy eyes. Very fortunately, we found that she had seen the *xebec* heave up her anchor and move towards a creek in-shore. The old man refused to leave his post, but his bright-eyed daughter, in the broken " lingua Franca," volunteered to guide us. Her offer was at once eagerly accepted by our " old man," who, however, seemed to have become dazed, as it were, in her presence. The rough tar had not often been brought into contact with such feminine beauty. Although her father seemed rather doubtful and uneasy, our solemn assurances, and the promise of a large reward, pacified him and obtained his consent. Descending to our boat, the young woman guided us to the mouth of a small creek at the southern extremity of the bay, and there, sure enough, close in under the tall rushes of the bank, lay the object of our chase. There was no fear of any mistake, for I had taken particular notice of several peculiarities in her build and rig.

THE XEBEC IN HIDING.

"Now then, my lads, are your arms all loaded, capped, and ready?" asked the captain.

"Ay, ay, sir," came in response; and the click, click, clicking of musket and pistol locks followed, whilst cutlasses were unsheathed and gripped by brawny hands.

"Luff up, then, Mister Leachline; luff up, and run her aboard," cried the "old man" to our mate, who was at the tiller.

As we closed with the brig, he continued—

"Now then, my hearties, don't forget what you are to do. Directly we get alongside, I and the second mate will make for the cabin, while all the rest of you—except Joe, who will remain in the boat and make her fast, and take care of the young woman —spring aboard the pirate, form a line across her decks abaft the mainmast, and keep her crew from coming aft. Mr. Leachline will command you."

The next moment we bumped alongside, and were scrambling over the Greek's low bulwarks.

The cordon was drawn across her decks, then I, the captain, and one of our men, who spoke Italian, entered her cabin, pistol and cutlass in hand.

As we did so, a figure sprang from the port state-room, and fired a pistol full in our faces.

"Cut him down, boys, cut him down!" roared the skipper, whose go-ashore hat had been mortally wounded by the ball.

I was nearest to our assailant, and before he could re-enter the berth from which he had appeared, I disabled him with a pretty sharp cut on the right shoulder, and then tumbled him over by dashing the hilt of my cutlass against his forehead.

At the same moment Captain Dobson entered the starboard or

right-hand berth—in every vessel that of her commander—and caught sight of the Greek skipper just getting up, aroused from his sleep by the noise, and attempting to hide the proceeds of the robbery he had committed earlier in the evening.

The unfortunate wretch had just withdrawn the swollen leather bag from underneath his pillow, when the iron grip of our "old man" was upon him. He made a vain effort to get at his long knife, but Captain Dobson took care of that. Then, first securing his lost money in one of his capacious pockets, he seized the Greek by the nape of the neck and the hinder part of his scanty clothing, and so ran him up the cabin stairs on deck.

"Philee-ee-p!" cried the piratical Grecian, as he went swiftly and unpleasantly through his cabin.

But his cry for help only elicited a lugubrious groan, for "Philee-ee-p," his mate, was lying somewhere under the cabin table, holding on to his wounded arm.

An extraordinary scene took place when we got on deck again. Handing over his victim for me to hold until he was ready, Captain Dobson stripped off his upper clothing, gave the bag of money into our mate's charge, and then told our man, who spoke Italian, to tell the Greek to stand up and defend himself.

The fellow understood what was required of him well enough, and his black eyes glared ferociously as his right hand instinctively made futile movements to where, no doubt, he usually carried the formidable stiletto, now safely stowed away in one of his enemy's pockets.

"Come on, you parley-woo, long-shore son of a sea-cook!" yelled our "old man." "Come on, will you, you murdering, piratical, inhospitable lubber! Come on, till I take satisfaction out of your black, ugly, skulking carcase!"

As our skipper squared up to him, the wretched Grecian cast a glance to where his crew were held completely at bay by the gleaming weapons of our men, then he sprang upon his antagonist, endeavouring to dash one fist in his face, and seize him by the throat with his other hand.

The poor wretch's pugilistic knowledge was sadly at fault, and he received a sound thrashing. He lay still at last; all resistance had been knocked out of him.

"Well, you plundering foreign vagabond, I've given you fair play," said the "old man;" "now I'll teach you to beware of interfering with a British skipper

THE LIGHTHOUSE KEEPER'S DAUGHTER.

again, for you're not going to dodge punishment by lying down like that.   Here, Jack, pass me the end of that main-brace."

Dear, dear, what a rope's-ending that Grecian skipper did receive! He must have been black, blue, and tender for a couple of months at least.   Such a terrible flagellation I never saw before or after.   He was almost naked, too !

At last Captain Dobson was satisfied, and ordered us into the boat.   Before daylight we were safely on board the *Mary Jane*, and things settled down again as though such an adventure had never occurred.

Within a week we were loaded and under-weigh for Liverpool, having heard no more of the affair.   The Greek captain, no doubt, had good reason for not troubling the authorities on shore.

As the brig was his own property, Captain Dobson was able to take her where he pleased, and I have heard that he went back to Taganrog more than once after the incident described; there was a great and unusual attraction at that grey old lighthouse.   I have heard, too, that a Russian Finn is keeper of it now, and that its former master, with his dark-eyed daughter leaning between him and a stalwart, fair-haired mariner, has been seen on board a certain British brig.   Well, she was a good-looking girl.   No wonder old Dobson thought it a capital opportunity to take a partner in the *Mary Jane*.   To see her in her smart native dress, which gave, perhaps, grandeur to a perfect figure, would have gone far to captivate a much more practised ladies' man than Captain Dobson.

THE LAST OF THE MUD-BANK.

THE LOG.

"THE Log of the *Fortuna*" is filled up. On the morning of January the 14th the brave little schooner floated (as our *Lowder* had predicted) once more upon her native element; and now we venture to cast her log-book adrift upon the troubled floods of literature, only trusting that all hands may be satisfied.

That last evening—properly speaking morning—of the yarn-spinning was a jovial one. After supper was dispatched, and after the conclusion of Esmond's second tale, we sang songs till daylight appeared, and the high tide floated the *Fortuna* off the mud-bank upon which we had spent so many days, that the proposed cruise had to be abandoned; the doctor and Mr. Lawrence being anxious to return to their respective occupations, whilst I was now in a great hurry to get back to Manilla, settle the business there, and return to the bosom of my wife and family.

Directly Esmond found that his tidy little craft was fairly under-weigh again, we had a parting glass all round, and then turned in to obtain a couple of hours' sleep before Ningpo hove in sight; leaving the mud-bank to the fast rising waves of the Chinese seas, and the wild sea-birds diving after their breakfasts, eddying and gyrating round about the last uncovered portion of our late resting-place.

THE END.

CASSELL, PETTER, AND GALPIN, BELLE SAUVAGE WORKS, LONDON, E.C.
671